Reunited for the Holidays

Jillian Hart

Love Inspired

Special thanks and acknowledgment are given to Jillian Hart
for her contribution to the Texas Twins miniseries.

Recycling programs
for this product may
not exist in your area.

™ LOVE INSPIRED BOOKS

ISBN-13: 978-0-373-81661-3

REUNITED FOR THE HOLIDAYS

www.LoveInspiredBooks.com

Printed in U.S.A.

"You may have to trust me to handle the situation," Brian said.

"Together, you and I made the decision to separate the twins in the first place," Belle said. "We'll make what decisions we have to now together. We're no longer married. You can't make decisions for me, Brian."

"Not that I ever could."

"No."

"I have no doubt when it comes to you, Isabella."

"I go by Belle now." How was she going to deal with Brian on an extended basis? With prayer and God's grace.

His gaze fastened on hers, betraying another hint of feeling. He gave a half smile, as if he remembered their married years, raising two sets of twins together. Toddling boys playing in the tiny house they rented. The warm, dear sounds of the babies awakening from their naps in the warm house decorated for Christmas.

Such good memories. Bright enough to outshine the bad.

* * *

Texas Twins: Two sets of twins, torn apart by family secrets, find their way home.

Books by Jillian Hart

Love Inspired

*A Soldier for Christmas
*Precious Blessings
*Every Kind of Heaven
*Everyday Blessings
*A McKaslin Homecoming
  A Holiday to Remember
*Her Wedding Wish
*Her Perfect Man
  Homefront Holiday
*A Soldier for Keeps
*Blind-Date Bride
†The Soldier's Holiday Vow
†The Rancher's Promise
  Klondike Hero
†His Holiday Bride
†His Country Girl
†Wyoming Sweethearts
  Mail-Order Christmas Brides
    "Her Christmas Family"
†Hometown Hearts
*Montana Homecoming
*Montana Cowboy
*Montana Dreams
††Jingle Bell Bride
  Reunited for the Holidays

Love Inspired Historical

*Homespun Bride
*High Country Bride
In a Mother's Arms
  "Finally a Family"
**Gingham Bride
**Patchwork Bride
**Calico Bride
**Snowflake Bride

*The McKaslin Clan
†The Granger Family Ranch
**Buttons & Bobbins
††The McKaslins of Wyoming

JILLIAN HART

grew up on her family's homestead, where she helped raise cattle, rode horses and scribbled stories in her spare time. After earning her English degree from Whitman College, she worked in travel and advertising before selling her first novel. When Jillian isn't working on her next story, she can be found puttering in her rose garden, curled up with a good book or spending quiet evenings at home with her family.

And let the peace of God rule in your hearts.
—*Colossians* 3:15

Chapter One

Dr. Brian Wallace plucked the ceramic frog out of the flower bed, tipped it upside down and shook hard. The spare front-door key fell onto his palm as he squinted into the watery afternoon sun. It was good to be home. Late November air crisped over him and he shivered, goose bumps traveling down his arms. Weak from an extended illness, he gripped the railing to steady himself. The long trip from rural Texas had taken a toll on him.

The old adage There's No Worse Patient Than a Doctor had never been more true, he thought, as he struggled up the stairs. Easily winded, he paused a moment at the top, thanking God he was here to see the colors of sunset. His near brush with death had marked him. He couldn't deny it. He'd missed his life here in Fort Worth.

He missed his kids—although they were grown, they were what he had left of his heart.

He ambled to the door, leaned heavily against the wall and inserted the key. The door creaked open. Every part of him vibrated with a mix of weakness and exhaustion. As he crossed the threshold into the comfort of the house, memories surrounded him. It had been years since his children had lived here, but he recalled the pound of music from an upstairs bedroom, the chatter of his daughter on her phone, the drum of feet as one of the boys prowled the kitchen.

Emotion dug into his chest, claws sharp. Yes, looking death in the face changed a man. It stripped away everything extraneous, leaving what mattered most.

His footsteps echoed in the lonely living room. He eased onto a couch cushion, sighing heavily as fatigue washed over him like water. Maybe he should have listened to his colleague—he'd valued Dr. Travors's expertise, which had saved his life—but he'd had enough bed rest. He needed to get home; he needed to be here. The Lord had put a deep call into his heart. He couldn't explain it as he reached for the phone to try his children again. He needed to see them.

He dialed his daughter's number first. Dear Maddie. Many things had crossed his mind while he'd lain on a spare cot in the corner of a migrant worker's temporary home—a shack beside many others on a remote Texas farm. His failings and regrets hit hard, but none as cruelly as his missteps in his personal relationships. He'd always had a difficult time opening up. He had to try to fix that. He'd been given a second chance.

He waited for the call to connect. A muffled ringing came from what sounded like his front porch. The bell pealed, boots thumped on the front step and joy launched him from the couch. He set down the phone, listening to the faint conversation on the other side of the door. His kids were here? Theirs were the voices he'd missed during his illness, the ones he'd most longed to hear. He gripped the brass knob, tugged and set eyes on his children. All three of them.

Praise the Lord, for bringing them here safe and sound. "You got my messages."

"You left about a dozen." Maddie tumbled into his arms. "Dad, you have no idea how good it is to see you. No idea."

"Right back at you, sweetheart." The endearment stumbled off his tongue—he wasn't good with them—but he had to get better at speaking his feelings. He had to try harder. His dear Maddie, so like her mother. His chest ached with affections too intense to handle, so he swallowed hard, trying to tamp them down as he held her hands in his after their hug was done. "I was gone a little longer than I'd planned this time—"

"A little?" Her voice shot up. "Dad, you have no idea how worried sick we've been over you."

"I don't even know how to say how sorry I am—"

"What matters is that you're all right." Her hands gave his a warm, understanding squeeze.

"Where have you been?" Grayson, his oldest child, stepped in to join the reunion. Tall, dark and handsome. Pride swelled up, making it hard to look at the boy properly.

"Grayson." Those couldn't be tears in his eyes, of course not. Brian wasn't a man given to tears. Maybe because he had thought of his two other children when he'd been fighting for his life on that cot. Yet another son and daughter, lost to him forever. His biggest regret of all. Emotion clumped in his throat, making it impossible to say more.

"We've been looking for you." Grayson's hug was brief, his face fighting emotion, too. "We found your wallet in a ditch and we feared you were missing. The police—"

"Missing?" He swiped a hand over his face, grimacing, hating what he'd put them through. "I was in rural Texas, you know that, sometimes without phones or cell service. I would have gotten a message to you kids, but I lost my cell—"

"I know. We found your phone, too." Carter, his youngest from his second marriage, stepped in, healthy and whole, back from war. "We were afraid you'd gotten ill. Are you all right, Dad?"

"Now I am." He wrapped his arms around Carter, holding him tight. When he ended the hug, he held on, drinking in the sight of the boy—okay, he was twenty-three, but Carter would always be his youngest, a seasoned soldier home from deployment safely. When Brian let go, it was hard to see again. He was grateful to God for returning his youngest son home unharmed.

"We heard you caught a virulent strain of strep." Carter ambled into the living room, making himself at home.

"And that you'd been treating a family who were dangerously ill." Grayson headed straight for the couch.

"We feared the worst, Dad." Beautiful Maddie with her auburn hair and a stylish fashion sense swept through the doorway, anguish carved into her dear face.

"I never meant to worry you." He shut the door, swallowing hard. His case had been severe and there'd been days, even weeks, where it hadn't been certain he would live. He didn't know what to do with the emotions coiled in his chest, so he shrugged, tried to play things down. "I survived, so it wasn't so bad."

"This is just like you. Always keeping us out instead of letting us in." Maddie sounded upset, on the verge of anger or tears, maybe both.

He hated upsetting her. Frustrated at himself, he crossed his arms over his chest. *Remember your vow, Brian. You have to try harder.* "I didn't mean it that way, honey. There's nothing to worry about now. I'm on the mend. That you kids are here, that you came, means everything."

It wasn't easy, but he got out the words.

"Oh, Daddy." Maddie swiped her eyes. "Don't you dare make me cry. I'm choked up enough already."

"What do you mean? What's got you choked up? Is something going on?"

"Dad, you'd better sit down for this." Grayson patted the seat beside him.

"This can't be good." He studied Carter's serious face and the troubled crinkles around Grayson's eyes. "Something happened while I was gone. That's why you were trying to reach me?"

"It's not bad news, but it could give you a real shock." Grayson cleared his throat, waiting until Brian eased onto the cushion. "There's no easy way to say this, so I'm just going to do it. We found Mom."

"Uh…" Brian's brain screeched to a halt, unable to make sense of those words. He was hearing things. No doubt due to his exhaustion and weakened state. "Sorry…say that again? Your mom's buried. She died when Carter was three. You remember the car accident."

"Not Sharla, Dad. Our real mother, at least for Grayson and me," Maddie added.

"Your real…? *What?*" That's as far as he got. The mention of the mother of his other son and daughter floored him. How could they know? All they could remember was Sharla, his second wife, the woman he'd married when the kids were very young. "Wait a minute. I don't understand. You're not making any sense."

"I know it's a shock for you, Daddy." Maddie settled on the couch across from him. "But it's true. Take a deep breath. I found our birth mother."

"No." He shook his head, refusing to see how that was possible. The only person Maddie could be talking about was Isabella…his first wife, his high school sweetheart, the woman who'd broken his faith in true love.

"I found Violet—" she began.

"Violet?" He blinked, his brain spinning.

"Thanks to a lucky coincidence, Violet and I

came face-to-face in a coffee shop and I found Mom from there." Maddie's hands cradled his.

Isabella was gone, tucked away in the Witness Protection Program with their two other children, never to be seen again. Their lives depended on it. "My mind's playing tricks on me because I thought you said—"

"Yes, I did. Mom is in Grasslands, and we're all together. Violet and Jack, well, they used to be Laurel and Tanner."

Laurel? Tanner? He shuddered, fighting the memory welling up of the U.S. Marshal driving away in a black SUV. Isabella in the window, cradling a six-month-old in her arms, and a little chestnut-haired boy, just two, waving bye-bye.

He swallowed hard. His lost children were here, in Texas. In Grasslands? *Within driving distance?* All this time he'd grieved for them, missed them with his entire heart for twenty-five years and now the two sets of twins were reunited? They'd found one another?

No, he shook his head, refusing to believe it. It couldn't be true. The hardest thing he'd ever done was let them go. But he'd had to make an impossible choice to protect his family from unspeakable danger.

"We're together now, Dad." Maddie's happiness was real. Her hands around his were real. "The only one missing is you."

Her words finally sank in. Realization crashed over him like a cold ocean wave, washing away disbelief.

This was really happening. It wasn't a hallucination or fever, born from his illness. He rubbed his hand over his face, took a deep breath and willed his heart rate to slow.

"Isabella." For twenty-five years—nearly all of his adult life—he'd been without her. And for good reason, he'd told himself. He'd done his best not to think of her for over two decades. That's the way he wanted it.

How could he tell his kids that? Maddie with her delight, Grayson actually smiling and Carter relaxed and at peace. This was good news for them.

But it wasn't good news. He thought about the reason for their separation in the first place. Was it safe to reunite the twins? What about the murderous drug dealer they'd been hiding from? His stomach clenched tightly as he pressed his hands to his face, overwhelmed.

"Violet and Jack are waiting to meet you, Dad." Carter stood, holding out his hand. "C'mon. I'll drive you."

"Good, because I'm not steady." A lot had

changed in twenty-five years, but not his love for his kids—for *all* of his kids. He took Carter's hand. "Then let's go."

As for Isabella, he'd cross that bridge when he came to it. The last thing he wanted was to see her again.

"Mom, you don't have to be so stubborn."

"Me, stubborn?" Belle gripped her walker, refusing to give in to the limitations her head injury and consequent coma had left her with. She had work to do—work she missed back home on the ranch—and being cooped up in Ranchland Manor wasn't in her plans for much longer. "What makes you say that?"

"Oh, no reason." Violet, her beautiful, redheaded daughter, rolled her eyes. "Will you get in bed already?"

"I'm not sleepy." The evening was still lovely, with the big Texas sky stretching like a soft blue canvas. She missed horseback riding beneath that canopy with the wind on her face. She breathed in, longing for the tangy scent of grass and open prairie. The biggest problem with being stuck in this place was the walls. At forty-three, Belle lived a very active lifestyle and liked her wide-open spaces. Maybe that had to do with those early years when she'd been in hiding, when her children were small.

"Mom, you're here to heal, remember?" Jack, her handsome, strapping son, tugged around the armchair, so it would face the window instead of the bed. "Can you take it easy for once?"

"That would be against my better judgment."

"Do something because we ask, okay?" Jack took her elbow.

"Yeah, Mom, it won't kill you, right?" Violet's loving laughter filled the room.

"It might," she quipped, clunking the walker to a stop beside the armchair. Here came the hard part. She stopped her walker a few inches away, giving her just enough distance so that she would have to take a step on her own.

"Do you have to do everything the hard way?" Jack's dry humor washed over her, making it easy to push off from the walker and lurch toward the chair. His strong hand banded her elbow, assisting her. Violet caught her other arm and she plopped onto the cushion. Goal achieved.

"Next time, it will be two steps," she declared, determined to push along her recovery from what they hoped was a temporary deficit of motor functions.

"Next time, it better not be." Violet plucked Belle's hairbrush off the nightstand. "You don't know what we went through when you fell off your horse and had to be rushed to the hospital."

"Our world stopped turning." Gruff, Jack

turned away, striding fast to the window. He planted his hand on his hips, staring out at the courtyard, his whole body reverberating with emotion.

"I hate that you were worried." She hadn't been there to comfort them or to ease their troubles, because she'd been in a deep coma. It tore her apart. All she'd ever wanted was to be there for her children.

"Worried doesn't begin to describe it." Violet leaned in, brushing Belle's thick auburn hair. "Terrified."

"Heartsick," Jack groused.

"You waking up was the best thing that could have happened." Violet blinked dampness from her eyes.

"The doctors say you are a wonder, too, coming back to us with hardly any impairment." Jack didn't turn from the window, but his gratitude vibrated in his voice.

"Which I'm grateful to God for. He is good." Belle patted her daughter's arm, love brimming for them, her precious children. More grateful for them because of the two children she'd left behind. "My big problem is how do I convince the doctors to stop with the tests? That's what I want to know."

"Think of it this way," Violet suggested. "The quicker all the testing is done, the sooner you can recover. The faster you can recover, the sooner you can come home."

"Home." Nothing sounded as good. To be in her own bed, to sit in the peaceful quiet of her living room and watch the horses graze in the paddock. The restless wind, the crisp scent of fall-becoming-winter air, feeling the sun on her back as she walked through the fields. That's the medicine she needed right now. She'd never been one to sit around and let grass grow under her boots. "Any chance either of you can smuggle me out?"

"Funny." Violet moved around the chair, tackling the other side of Belle's hair. Across the room Jack's phone buzzed. He reached into his pocket to check the screen. When he did, he traded looks with Violet.

Significant looks. As if Violet fully understood, she set aside the brush.

"You're looking lovely, Mom." A quick squint, a frown, and then she brushed a shock of hair behind Belle's ear. "There. Absolutely stunning."

"Okay, what's up with you two? What are you not telling me? Don't even try to deny it, because I know that look." Belle couldn't explain why her pulse lurched into an unsteady gallop, as if she could feel a change in the air. "Where are Maddie and Grayson?"

"On their way." Jack's jaw tensed as he leaned back, resting on the windowsill.

"They should be here any minute." Violet's hands fumbled as she reached for a barrette. "One more touch, and you'll be perfect. Dad won't be able to catch his breath."

"Did you say— No, that's not right." Belle shook her head. Something had to be wrong with her brain because she'd thought she'd heard…

"Dad. I like the sound of that." Jack launched to his feet, facing the doorway. "It's good to meet you. So good."

Dad? A tall, well-built man towered just out of reach of the light. She blinked, trying to bring the shadow into focus, but she didn't need to see him to know his identity. Her heart leaped and tingles flickered down her spine in recognition. Tears burned behind her eyes as he strode into the light, whole and safe. Her ex-husband, more handsome than ever, and distinguished with a touch of gray in his dark hair. The last time she'd seen him, he'd been eighteen, nearly nineteen.

"Come in. It's so good to finally meet you." Violet dashed across the room and into her father's arms.

"You were just a little thing when I saw you last." Brian's voice, still familiar after all this time, sounded tortured with emotion. He blinked dampness from his eyes as he reached out to hold his son. Jack hesitated a moment, as if he were unsure, before stepping into his father's hug. "You were just a toddler, Jack. I would lay you on my chest and rock you until you fell asleep."

"I don't remember. Wish I did." Jack swallowed, obviously wrestling with emotion as he stepped back. Only then did she notice her other children—the exact duplicates of Violet and Jack—slipping into the room. Carter hung back, watching the reunion.

There had been a lot of reunions in this family lately. There was only one more left. She straightened her spine, bracing for it, while at the same time wishing there was some way to get out of facing her ex.

"Isabella." He choked on her name, frozen in place halfway to the bed, fisting his hands.

Maybe he was debating the merits of turning heel and leaving, so he didn't have to deal with her. Or perhaps he was just as shocked as she was with the reality of seeing him again.

There'd been a time when she had believed she'd never be in the same room with him. That there would be no possible way. Life could sure surprise you.

"Brian." She lifted her chin. No way was she going to let anyone know this was killing her. *Put on a smile,* she told herself, *and welcome him.* This was about the kids, not her. "You're looking well. I'm thankful for that. We've all feared for you."

"I understand the same can be said of you." A muscle ticked along his strong jaw. Time had matured him, drew character in his face and pleasant lines around his eyes. "It's good to see you."

She couldn't meet his gaze, although she could feel it sweep along her face. She tried to answer him, but words stuck in her throat and refused to budge. It wasn't good to see him again. It was agony.

"Maybe we should leave you two alone to talk," one of the girls suggested—maybe Maddie? Belle didn't dare look up to see for sure. Staring at a polished fingernail—the girls had given her a manicure this morning—gave her something to do as the kids left the room, calling out promises to talk later to Brian, that they couldn't wait to share the good news with their significant others. As their voices and footsteps faded, silence settled in—or what silence she could make out over the thump of her heart echoing in her ears.

Brain came closer, then halted again.

"You don't have to see me if you don't want to." His baritone turned tender and smoky, the way it always had when it had just been the two of them.

Images assailed her—of them standing side by

side at the boys' cribs while they slept. Of Brian bringing her a steaming cup of her favorite tea while she nursed newborn Grayson, with Tanner tucked in one of his arms. And less than two years later, of the pride and stark love on his face in the delivery room when they both drank in the sight of their beautiful newborn daughters. She could still feel his kiss to her forehead, so sweet her soul ached.

"It's fine." She found the courage she needed to meet his gaze. A stranger's gaze, she told herself stubbornly. That young man she'd loved— that teenager who'd stood beside her as husband and best friend—no longer existed. Just as she was no longer that same starry-eyed girl.

A lifetime separated them. And always would.

Chapter Two

"Come sit, Brian. You look pale." Belle might be trying to hide it, but he could sense her true feelings. All she wanted was for him to turn back around and walk out of her life.

He knew the feeling. It would have been easier if he'd never walked through that door.

"The kids have been worried." She looked toward the window instead of at him.

"I didn't know they were searching for me." His voice didn't sound like his own, so raw and broken. Too vulnerable, he sank into a bedside chair. "I was out of touch longer than I planned, but I was safe and cared for."

"You look exhausted. You always were one to work too hard."

"I used to work hard for you, Isabella. For our kids." He didn't expect her to understand the pride he felt in his family when they'd been teenage parents fighting to keep their marriage together. "I never meant to let you down."

There, he'd said it. The words he'd yearned to say since the U.S. Marshal drove her and two of their children away. "I'm sorry."

"I forgave you long ago." She bowed her head, not looking at him. "We both had to get on with our lives."

"Yes." He bowed his head, too. "Forgetting is a different matter."

"It was easier when I knew I'd never have to see you again."

"Easier to keep it buried." Those feelings of failure, the mountains of regret. So much lay lost and broken between them—marriage vows, promises and the hope of raising their kids together. "We each had kids to take care of. Protecting them came first."

"Exactly." She lifted her head, her soft auburn hair cascading over her shoulders with a graceful bounce.

"This really must be a shock for you. Seeing me like this. The twins didn't warn you I was coming?"

"No." She traced her fingertips along the edging of the armchair so she didn't have to look at him.

"I tried to prepare myself on the way here." He cleared his throat. Time had changed her—

her face had lost the round softness of youth, to be replaced by almost regal maturity that was impossibly more beautiful. But she was no longer his, and that's the way they both wanted it. "Carter told me all about how the twins found one another and how they were praying at your bedside on Thanksgiving when you first opened your eyes and came back to them."

"Carter is a wonderful young man. He's so much like you—" Her honest, unguarded gaze found his. This wasn't easy for her, either.

"I hope he doesn't make my mistakes."

"We all make mistakes." Regret weighed on her, too, easy to see. "I hear you are an amazing doctor, like I always knew you would be. You help people, Brian. You make a difference in this world, and your children are proud of you."

"You don't have to try so hard to be kind to me, Isabella. We didn't exactly part on good terms."

"No, but for the kids' sake—"

"We have to try." He nodded, glad they agreed on this. If only he knew what to do about the pain wedged into his chest. Seeing her again made him aware of how he'd failed her. Being teenage parents with two sets of twins had been tough and the stress had torn them apart. He'd been to blame for that. He couldn't deny it, and the guilt burdened him.

"They shouldn't be proud. I'm not saving the world, just going where God leads." His head reeled, more overwhelmed than he wanted to admit. "This latest mission didn't turn out like I expected. For a while I worried I might not see the kids again."

"Oh, Brian. That must have been agonizing. When I woke up and realized what I could have lost—"

"Exactly. Weddings. Grandchildren. Birthdays." He smiled wistfully. "Speaking of which, I couldn't believe it when I discovered that *all* of our kids are altar-bound."

"I had a similar reaction to the news," she confessed. "But deep down, I'm so thankful to God for both of our lives…and that we get to share in the happiest of our children's lives."

"I'm thankful *you're* here, Isabella. But for the Lord's grace, I might be having to confront our grieving children and I don't think I could take seeing them hurt like that."

"That was my fear, too." Her hand found his— large and strong—and at the touch of his skin, her heart twisted. The pain of the past and the divorce stood between them, refusing to relent. She swallowed hard, wishing the past didn't hurt so much. "What happened to you? Why couldn't the kids find you?"

"The strep hit hard. One moment I was fine, the next I was so sick I couldn't function...."

"Tell me everything," Belle insisted.

"I recall leaving Blackstone in my beat-up SUV and heading toward a farming town along the border. Unfortunately, my car overheated when I was ten miles outside the migrant camp."

"How awful! So you were stranded in the middle of nowhere with no cell phone?"

"It wasn't as bad as it sounds. A local farm worker happened by in his truck and arranged to have my car towed for repairs. Since it was on his way, he offered to drop me off at the migrant camp while my vehicle was being worked on." He sighed heavily. "Unfortunately, car troubles were the least of my worries. By the end of my first day at the migrant camp, I was sidelined by a cough and a high fever."

Belle couldn't hide her concern. "Oh, my... what happened next?"

"I knew I had to leave, because I could be highly contagious and might be doing more harm than good at the camp. So I got a lift back to the auto shop, picked up my SUV and decided to drive to a nearby medical clinic to get checked out." A shadow crossed his face. "But a short time later I had to pull over because I was too weak to drive and a hazard to others. I sat on the side of the road praying for someone to come by…and the next thing I knew, I woke up in the ditch."

"That must have been where they found your wallet."

"I hadn't realized I'd lost it. I'd passed out. It was night and I crawled my way through a field for miles toward a faint light. A house, as it turned out. The Cruz family took me in and cared for me." He took a deep breath, then continued. "Mr. Cruz took my keys and fetched my car after finding a doctor. I was barely conscious and they didn't have a phone, so I couldn't call home. I was too ill to write a letter. Those people saved my life."

"Bless them, and we're all grateful." Thankfulness filled her with such power it made her eyes burn. Thankfulness, for the kids' sake. She tore her hand from his. "Thank the Lord you were able to come back to be with your children."

She turned so he couldn't see her face. She didn't want him to guess how much this cost her. She wanted to be anywhere but with him. It hurt too much. She moved forward on the chair cushion, needing to get away.

"Let me help you, Isabella." His chair scraped.

"No, I'm fine." She pushed out of the chair, her left side sluggish. "I've got this."

"That doesn't mean you have to do it alone."

"It does." She'd been on her own for decades. She couldn't start leaning on him now. "The twins might be reunited, but that doesn't change anything between us."

"I didn't expect it would." His dark chocolate eyes gleamed with regret.

Regret she shared. Regret she felt all the way to her soul. The chasm of twenty-five years stood between them, a distance too great to bridge. Their love, once broken, couldn't be repaired. It just couldn't. "Seeing you again is harder than I predicted. It hurts."

"Yes." He covered his heart with the flat of his palm. "You would think all this time would have healed it."

"Or maybe numbed it a little."

"Exactly," he agreed. "But it hurts the way it did when you asked for a divorce, while our children slept in the next room."

"I remember." The night their marriage ended and they'd given up hope. She gripped the walker for support. Dismissing the doctor's orders not to be up on her own, she made her way shakily toward the window, hating the impairment that slowed her. Tamping down memories of one of the worst nights in her life wasn't easy. "We need to come to an agreement, Brian."

"What kind of agreement?"

"About you and me. How we deal with each other."

He swallowed painfully. "Right. Do you have any suggestions?"

"We do the only possible thing. Let's leave this in the past where it belongs and go on from here."

"If that's what you want." Traces of pain hid in his voice. "We've both been hurt enough."

"Yes." She clunked her walker forward and stepped purposefully. The arguments, the sleepless nights, the stress of being teenage parents with two sets of twins haunted her. She'd been shattered the night she'd asked Brian to leave. No way would she let him see that, so her chin went up with stubborn determination to hide her vulnerabilities.

"Glad we agree," he said gruffly.

"We have to get along for the children's sake."

"The big question is how."

"I have no idea." Her reflection in the dark window looked back at her. She saw a thin woman, hollow cheeked and fragile looking. Not the same vibrant Belle Colby who'd fallen off her horse. The coma and injury had ravaged her, but she was determined to regain her strength… and reclaim her life. She caught sight of Brian struggling to his feet and realized that she wasn't the only one ailing here. "We are quite a pair, aren't we?"

"We always have been." He shuffled toward her, fighting to stay tall and strong, but she could read the strain on his face, the tension along his carved jaw, even in the window's reflection. "Carter told me how this all came about, how Violet met Maddie. How the kids came together again. One thing has been eating away at me. I can't help wanting to protect my children. It can't be safe to reunite them, can it?"

"I've been worried about that, too," she said softly.

"What about—?"

"David Johnson, the man I testified against? Yes, he's still in prison, at least as far as I know. I haven't been well enough these past few days—"

"You just woke from a coma."

"Yes, but that doesn't mean I can't fear the worst. What if Johnson figures out where we are?"

"Exactly. He may be in jail, but he likely still has his contacts on the outside."

"The kids don't know about the danger. They don't remember going into hiding. They don't know why we moved from Forth Worth all those years ago, and I refuse to talk about it. That's what Jack and I argued about right before my accident. He wanted to know about you."

"It must have been hard not to tell him. You had to want to."

"I did." She appreciated that he understood. "It was too dangerous."

"When I remarried, Maddie and Grayson were young enough not to remember. That made the past disappear."

"Disappear?" She held herself steady, breathing as if in pain. "A mother never wants to be forgotten by her children."

"Neither does a father."

This pain they shared, a pain visible on his sculpted face. She couldn't believe her eyes. The honest display of his feelings surprised her. They'd already been divorced when she'd unknowingly stumbled into a dangerous situation. Their marriage had fallen apart because she'd been convinced he hadn't cared about her, at least not the way a husband should. Brian could be so unemotional, closed off, clinical in his relationships. To see him overcome like this, with the manly intake of breath, the gathering of his control as he straightened up, made her realize how much had changed. Emotions skittered across his face, no longer hidden to her.

"I never even considered we might be in this situation one day, with the twins reunited," he confessed. "All this time not knowing if you were safe or if they would be all right. The horrific nightmares I had of David Johnson escaping prison and hunting down the kids and there being nothing I could do. No matter what, we have to keep them safe."

"We will." That had never been in doubt. "I need to get in touch with my handler, but I've been stuck here with no one I can confide in."

"You have me." A smile touched his lips, chiseled and lean. The years hadn't changed that smile, masculine and bracketed by dimples. "That may not be any consolation, but I'll make sure our children are protected."

"We'll do it together." Gently, she reached out to brush a strand of hair from his eyes. An old habit, she realized too late. She respected her ex-husband and his love for their children, that was all. They were temporarily joining forces to safeguard their family, but when the dust settled, the old conflicts would still be between them.

"Are you sure you're up to this?" His emotions retreated, his eyes shuttered and he was closed off once again. His dark gaze gave nothing away. "You may have to trust me to handle the situation."

"Together, you and I made the decision to separate the twins in the first place." She winced, remembering the wrenching decision they'd been forced to make. "We'll make what deci-sions we have to together. Remember we are no longer married. You can't make decisions for me, Brian."

"Not that I ever could." A muscle jumped along his square jaw.

"No." Was he remembering their late-night ar-guments, too? Times best forgotten, she thought, straightening her spine. "The doctors tell me I'm frail, but I don't believe them. My memory is coming back, my speech is just fine, and before you know it, I'll be walking on my own steam out the front doors of Ranchland Manor."

"I have no doubt when it comes to you, Isa-bella."

"I go by Belle now." How was she going to deal with Brian on an extended basis? After all, they were bound to see a lot of each other since their children all wanted to reconnect as a fam-ily. "I hear what sounds like a herd of elephants in the hallway. Must be our kids."

"Must be." His gaze fastened on hers, betray-ing another hint of feeling. How had the years made him more handsome? His carved-granite face, high forehead, dark eyes and prominent cheekbones were flawless. He gave a half smile, as if he remembered their married years, raising two sets of twins together. Toddling boys playing in the small living room of the tiny house they'd rented. Childish voices rising in glee. "No! No! Mine! Mine! Boom!" as toys went flying and the boys' laughter rang. The dear sounds of the baby girls awakening from their naps in the warm house decorated for Christmas.

Such good memories. Bright enough to outshine the bad.

"Mom! Dad." All grown up, Violet bounded in, leading the group back from the cafeteria. "You two look cozy. Don't you think?" she asked her sister.

"Absolutely." Maddie's grin shone triumphantly. "Looks like we came back too soon. Maybe we all should head to the cafeter—"

"Don't you dare walk off." Belle used her Mom voice. "I'm still in charge around here."

"So you think." Jack set a steaming cup of tea on the bedside table while everyone laughed.

"Hello? Hello?" A knock rapped on the open door and a nurse hustled in. "So glad to see y'all here, but visiting hours are over. You'll be back bright and early tomorrow, I suppose?"

"Count on it." Violet circled the end of the bed. "Mom, what did the doctor say?"

"Hmm, let me think. I can't quite remember," she hedged.

"Wasn't it something like stay in bed? You are still recovering, Mom." Maddie swooped in and caught Belle's other elbow. "Is she always this much trouble, Violet?"

"Usually more."

"Hey!" Belle argued good-naturedly as she let them help her to her feet. "I'm not an invalid. I can manage on my own."

"This sounds very familiar." Brian's baritone lifted above the other conversations as Grayson pulled aside the bedcovers and Jack plumped her pillows. "I see some things haven't changed."

"Brian is talking about my stubbornness, in case you kids couldn't guess." She eased onto the mattress. "I don't think I'm stubborn."

"Sure, of course you're not," Violet teased. "Not one of us has ever thought that."

The entire room laughed. Even Belle.

"Sleep well, Mom." Maddie kissed her forehead.

"Sweet dreams." Violet kissed her cheek and stepped back.

"We'll see you in the morning, Mom." Grayson squeezed her hand.

"We love you." Jack drew up her covers.

"I love you all. That means you, too, Carter."

"Back at ya, Belle." Carter smiled at her before stepping away and offering his arm to his father. "I'll bring Dad tomorrow to visit."

"Excellent." She hated how exhausted Brian looked. He'd been without family, fighting a dangerous illness. What if he'd passed away? He never would have known each twin he'd given up was now safe.

"Have a good night, Isabella—Belle," he corrected, standing on his own, refusing his son's aid. He looked even paler, if that were possible.

"You, too, Brian. We'll talk again tomorrow."

"Count on it." He hesitated, as if about to say something, but stayed silent. He raised a hand in a show of farewell.

She raised hers. Tomorrow, she'd have to face him again.

"Just lie back, Mom." Violet fussed over her, blowing on her tea and moving her Bible within easy reach on the nightstand.

"Is there anything else you need?" Maddie asked.

Such good girls. Seeing those identical faces brought tears to her eyes. Behind them, at the doorway, the boys lingered, checking in on her one last time before waving and stepping out of sight.

"Just take good care of Brian." She sank into the pillows, grateful to relax. She could pretend all she wanted that she was just fine, but that wasn't entirely true. The coma and head injury had taken a lot out of her, and it would be a while before she was back to her old, feisty self.

"We'll look after Dad, I promise." Maddie stepped away first, the vow shining in her eyes.

When the girls left, they seemed to take the light with them. Still, she smiled to herself as she heard Violet and Maddie lingering outside the door, gushing about how this was going to be the best Christmas ever. Not only did they have Landon and Ty—their doting fiancés—in their lives, but now their entire family was finally all together.

Belle heard their footsteps retreat down the hall and silence settled in—the way it had on the night she'd ordered Brian out of their little house and, later, on the first night she'd been in protective custody, listening to the children sleep and wondering about the other half of the twins in Brian's care.

Brian. The kids had thought it was a great surprise for her to see him tonight, but they didn't know the agony it brought.

Give me strength, Lord. She tugged her Bible into her arms and hugged it to her heart. *Most of all, please keep our children safe.*

"You look happier, Dad." Carter helped him into the passenger side of the truck. "Seeing Belle was good for you."

"I don't know about that." He cleared his throat, collapsed into the seat and did his best to cover up how hard seeing Belle had been—and would continue to be. "You kids sure surprised her, too. I'm not certain that was a fair thing to do to a woman who spent five months in a coma."

"During which she murmured your name. I heard it." Carter drew himself up, hardly more than a shadow in the night. "I hadn't felt a connection to her until then and I realized she loves you. That's all I needed to know."

"Belle doesn't love me. At least she hasn't for a long, long time." That was his fault, failings that tore him up.

"You never know what God has in store." Carter stepped back, hand on the door, preparing to swing it shut. "There's still something between you two, I think."

Yes, there was—animosity, bitterness and remorse. The door closed with a click, leaving Brian alone in the cab. Grateful for that, he tried to gather his strength, watching Carter cross the pavement to exchange words with Grayson. The kids were climbing into their vehicles, waving goodbye, calling out plans for tomorrow, leaving him time alone to think.

Isabella—Belle—looked more beautiful than ever. No surprise she'd done so well without him. She'd always been strong and independent-minded. She'd rebuilt her life, raised two of their children and run a successful ranch. Turned out she'd never needed him the way he'd needed her.

How was he going to be able to face her tomorrow? And the day after that? This matter of David Johnson was a big one. Belle had risked her life in order to put the drug-dealing criminal away.

Horns honked in friendly beeps, and he waved as the kids drove off—Maddie and Violet together in Violet's SUV, Jack and Grayson in separate vehicles. A sight he'd never thought he would see in his life—the kids reunited, laughing and gleeful, dreaming of a future filled with love and happiness.

That's the way he wanted to keep it. Tomorrow, first thing, he and Belle had to figure out a way to keep their children safe.

"Dad, are you okay?" Carter settled behind the wheel, concern furrowing his forehead.

"Just tired. It's been a long day." He relaxed against the headrest. "There's one more thing I need to do. Is there a church around?"

"Grasslands Community Church isn't far from here." Carter started the engine and buckled up. "Do you want to stop by?"

"Yes."

Carter pulled out his cell phone. "Let me just make a quick call to let Savannah know we'll be home a little late." He smiled indulgently. "My lovely fiancée tends to worry, especially with all those pregnancy hormones running amok."

Brian beamed back at Carter. He'd heard how his youngest son had taken his fallen comrade's pregnant wife under his wing—and fallen in love in the process. He couldn't be prouder of his boy.

The ride was a short one. The church door stood open as a late Bible study was just disbanding, from what Brian could overhear in the parking lot. He left Carter in the truck and climbed the stairs. His movements rustled in the empty sanctuary, where the stained-glass windows gazed down at him darkly. God's presence surrounded him, a calm that strengthened his weary body and refreshed his hurting soul.

"Dear Heavenly Father," he began, kneeling, his voice echoing slightly in the shadows. "As You know, I've been absent from worship lately when I was ill and I've missed it sorely. Thank You for sparing my life. I know it was a near thing, and I'm more grateful than ever after tonight. Seeing the twins reunited and Belle—"

He stopped, struggling to clear the lump in his throat. Belle, more beautiful than ever. Just as stubborn and full of grit, her smile could light up a room the way it once had lit every chamber of his heart. "You answered my only prayer. That somehow, someway, I could see my lost children again. That they could all find happiness together, reunited, the way it should have been. Thank You, Father, from the bottom of my heart. Please hold them safe in the palm of Your hand."

His amen echoed in the stillness and peace. As Brian climbed to his feet, he felt God's touch like a ray of hope in the dark late November night.

Chapter Three

The first day of December shone bright and beautiful. Belle followed the path of sunshine tumbling into the corridor along Ranchland Manor's tiled floors with maddeningly slow speed.

"Up again?" Helga, one of the nurses, looked up from her station. "I thought the doctor wanted you to rest."

"Think of this as an extra physical therapy session." Belle trudged by. "The faster I recover, the sooner I can leave. No offense, Helga."

"None taken."

"But we'll miss you, dearie." Eunice Lundgrin looked up from her crocheting as Belle entered the large, bright common room. "You liven things up around here."

"Only since I've been out of my coma," Belle quipped over the thunk of her walker. "Don't tell me you ladies finished the jigsaw puzzle without me."

"You didn't think we'd wait for you, did you?" Marjorie Collins looked up from her book. "You left us to go see that handsome Kirk."

"He's a physical therapist and my son's age!" Laughing, Belle eased into the overstuffed chair closest to the picture window, aching to be outside in wide-open spaces. "It wasn't a date."

"Pretty girl like you ought to have a fella." Eunice completed her double crochet with a flourish.

"I tried that once and discovered it wasn't for me." Laughing was easier than the truth of how hard marriage had been as teenage parents. She shot the older ladies a smile. "Men are just too much trouble."

"I can't say they aren't," Anna Chandro piped in as she reached the end of her knitted row, making lovely progress in spite of her stroke. "My Roberto, God rest his soul, was more trouble than I knew what to do with. Most days he was like having another kid around."

"Ain't that the truth?" Eunice agreed, giving her yarn ball a tug. "I raised my Charlie right along with our four boys. He was always tracking mud in on his shoes, forgetting to pick up his towel, turning up the TV volume until a girl couldn't think."

"I would have taken a broom to him," Marjorie teased, marking her page and closing her inspirational romance novel. "My John doesn't dare step one toe out of line."

"Oh, yes, I saw it in his eyes when he visited yesterday." Belle couldn't help giving a little sigh. The dear lady's room was across the hall from hers, and she'd spotted the wizened John arriving with a bouquet of flowers, a stack of new novels, and he'd stayed to share supper with her in the dining room. A sweeter couple never lived. Lifelong love, that had once been her dream, too…and no, she wasn't going to let her heart flutter at the mention of his name.

"Speaking of guests, I saw Mr. Tall, Dark and Handsome leave Belle's room quite late last night."

"Is that right?" Eunice gave her yarn another good yank. "So, there seems to be a lot Belle isn't telling us. Look at her blush."

"I'm not blushing. It's the heat. I'm sitting in the direct sun." Denial was always her first coping choice, along with a quick change of subject. "My children visited again last night, that's all."

"We noticed," Eunice said, crocheting with lightning speed. "How could we not? Those two sets of twins?"

"They're adorable." Marjorie smiled, her hand

resting on her book. "The girls are both so lovely, such nice, well-behaved young ladies."

"And those boys, strapping and handsome." Anna's needles stilled. "What I can't figure is how you managed with two sets of twins. One newborn is a handful. Up most of the night between feedings, diapers and colic. How did you handle twins? And *twice?*"

"It wasn't easy, especially since I was sixteen at the time." The confession came quietly, since she wasn't sure how the older women would take her news. "Brian and I married and had the twin boys. The girls came two years later."

"Double the blessings, double the hard work," Eunice sympathized.

"And the stress. Child care is the most demanding work there is," Marjorie piped in gently. "Four little ones all two years old or younger. I couldn't have survived it. Stress would have done me in. Just proves you're one special lady, Belle."

"You are way too kind." Belle's chest knotted up as it always did, thinking of those years. Failure haunted her. She hadn't been the wife and the mother she'd meant to be.

"Anyone can see you did a wonderful job," Anna added lovingly.

"You three are the wonderful ones. No wonder we've become fast friends." Belle felt a change in the air and turned toward the doorway where

Brian stood. How long he'd been listening in was anyone's guess.

"Good afternoon, ladies." Brian tossed them a dazzling smile.

He looked better this morning. A good night's sleep had done him wonders. He had more color in his face, and the dark circles were gone. The wind had tousled his dark hair, giving him a slightly rakish look, a reminder of the young man she'd fallen irrevocably in love with.

Not that she ever could again, she thought, wishing the other women in the room weren't giving him a collective sigh of approval. Trying not to imagine what her new friends would be saying next, she spoke up before they could. "I thought you were going to take some time for yourself. Rest up. Regain your strength."

"I'm tough. I don't need to rest." His easygoing humor rolled over her, just like in the old days.

But those days are long gone, she reminded herself stubbornly. Besides, as the kindly older ladies had reminded her, she wouldn't want to go back. Their marriage hadn't worked. End of story. She struggled to her feet. "I'm not sure what to do with you, Brian Wallace."

"It's too late to pretend you don't know me."

"Don't think it didn't cross my mind." Before she could stand fully, he was at her side, his hand cradling her elbow, keeping her steady as he dragged her walker closer for her.

Her independent streak flared. It would be prudent to let him know straight off she didn't need his help, now or ever. But that wasn't fair to him. He was only trying to be courteous. Brian was simply being Brian.

"Thank you." The words felt strangled. His nearness washed over her like sunshine—bright, refreshing and enlivening. Things she didn't want to feel again, not when it came to Brian. She grasped the walker's grips and shuffled forward, aware of him tall and straight at her side.

Her limitations frustrated her. As grateful as she was to have survived a head injury and resulting coma, she wanted to ride her horse, jog at her usual breakneck speed and keep up with things at the ranch. Worse, she hated being vulnerable around Brian when she needed to be strong.

"Don't they make the cutest couple?" Eunice cooed.

"The cutest," Marjorie agreed, opening her book.

"They look like they belong together," Anna sighed as her knitting needles began clacking again.

She lumbered across the room as fast as possible. Was Brian upset also by that last comment? The two of them used to belong together.

Used to. Not anymore. That was something that would never change.

"I spent most of the morning on the phone." He pitched his voice low, so it wouldn't carry in the busy hallway. "The marshal who handled you—"

"Tommy Hatfield." Fondness swept through her. Tommy had been good to her and her children, a rock when she'd feared for their lives. "How is he?"

"Retired. When I couldn't reach him at his office, I tried his home phone."

"They gave you that information?"

"No, I already had it. Did you think I would let you go without a single worry? Without making sure I knew the man who was taking you and the kids into protective custody?" A muscle jumped along his jaw, betraying his quiet words.

"I never gave it any thought."

"You had a lot on your mind at the time." His tone was kind as he matched his gait to her halting one. *Kind* was one adjective that had always described Brian. *Committed* was another. "Before he took you, I grilled that man. I had to make sure he'd done every possible thing to keep the three of you out of harm's way. I couldn't rest until I was certain of it."

"I didn't know."

"You weren't supposed to."

It shamed her. At the time she'd been convinced Brian had fallen out of love with her so thoroughly, he didn't care one iota for her. She should have considered his feelings more, the ones that may have lurked out of sight behind his unemotional exterior.

Maybe, she admitted, she should have voiced her concern and her caring for him more during their troubled marriage. It was too late to fix it, so she swallowed, concentrating on trudging forward, blind to where they were going.

"Tommy's wife gave me his cell number, and I caught him out fishing." Brian stopped to pull out a chair for her. "He sounded pretty surprised to hear from me. He didn't know anything new about your case, so he has to get back to me."

"So, more waiting." She plunked into the offered chair, hardly noticing the dining room echoing around her. The vacant tables, the sounds of the staff hard at work in the kitchen, the rustle of Brian's clothes as he drew out a chair and sat beside her, facing her, so close she could see the threads of bronze in the melted-chocolate color of his irises.

That kindness she read there hadn't changed. He was still such a good man. Caring and compassionate. She hoped he'd found happiness in his life. Their failed marriage had been only half his fault.

"What do we tell the kids?" He leaned forward, his elbows on his knees.

"All of it. If my argument with Jack taught me anything, it's that lies can destroy a family."

"That's right…you'd mentioned that you'd gotten into an intense confrontation with Jack before you fell off your horse."

"He wanted to know who his father was, once and for all, and he was furious when I refused to tell him." She couldn't remember the argument or even hitting the ground. The details of that day were fuzzy to nonexistent, but it hadn't been the first argument they'd had on the subject. She leaned back in the chair. "Don't think I'd forgotten you or forgot the father Jack and Violet should have had."

He swallowed hard, nodded once, obviously unable to answer. Guilt and sadness moved across his face.

Interesting. Yet again she was reminded that the Brian Wallace she'd once known hadn't been one to show feelings at all, even in the heat of an argument. But now… She could detect a flicker of raw emotion in his eyes.

"There has always been a huge gaping hole in my life. In our lives." His confusion sounded gruff, a father who'd been forced to walk away from two of his children. "It tore me apart."

"Me, too." Tears stung her eyes and she blinked them away, refusing to let them fall. Brian spotted them and leaned in to lay his hand against her cheek. One tear rolled across her skin and into the cup of his palm. The pain she felt, the wrenching agony of the hole in her life where he, Maddie and Grayson should have been, eased. "I never stopped missing them."

"Me, either. I can get to know Violet and Jack, although I keep wanting to call them by their original names, before the marshal changed them. It's going to take some getting used to."

"It took me a long time to get used to it, too," she admitted softly. "As important as it was at the time, I kept slipping up. Violet was just a baby, so she adjusted to her name easier, but Jack kept stubbornly insisting he was Tanner. We had to make a game of it."

"I can picture it. Grayson cried and cried for you. Night after night, day after day. Being alone when he'd been with his twin every hour of the day and night didn't help. He cried for Tanner— I mean, Jack—too."

"I wondered." She gazed upon his face, the one she knew so well. The memory of him had stayed with her more than she'd realized. "I ached for them every night and day. They were my children."

"Being separated from them was torture. It would have been easier to reach in and cut out my heart. I knew you felt the same way." Understanding shone in his eyes. He'd walked in those shoes, too.

Maybe dealing with Brian won't be so bad, she thought. He'd been hurt, too. God willing, maybe the hurting was over. "I really think we can go on from here. We can be civil, right?"

"Right. For the children's sake." He moved away as if they'd never been close, as if they were just two people sitting together, side by side in a big empty room. The clunk and clatter from the kitchen echoed loudly. "We keep them safe, we work together to make sure the past doesn't harm them and once this is over, I'll be on my way."

"Back to Fort Worth?"

"That's where my life is." His home, his practice, his church, his friends. "I'll be back for the weddings, of course. But don't worry, Belle, you won't have to deal with me for long."

"That's not what I was worrying about." For an instant, a hint of vulnerability softened her Cupid's-bow mouth, and in the brush of sunlight tumbling through the wide windows, she looked bronzed, the highlights in her auburn hair gleaming like rare silk, and a flashback from the past roared through him—the image of Belle sitting in the rocking chair, one newborn cradled in each arm, serene and glowing with a new mother's love. Affection he'd thought was long dead whispered in his heart, just ashes of what was, he rationalized. That's all it could be. His love for her had died long ago, but his caring for her hadn't.

That caring was what motivated him now. He launched off his chair and held out his hand. "Let's check you out of here and get you a real meal."

"What does that mean? A homemade meal?"

"Sure, in some restaurant. We'll find one."

"I'll text my housekeeper, Lupita, and have the kids bring a meal from the ranch. A big picnic lunch for all of us." She eased off her chair, her left leg weak. At least she allowed him to help. "We can eat it in the sunroom, although it's strange to think it's December. I still look outside and expect it to be hot, sunny July."

"A lot of time passed while you were sleeping."

"And a lot of things changed. Like the fact that our kids are suddenly all madly in love. I just wish I had been here to see them find their perfect soul mates." Her chin hiked up, full of grit. "And did I mention I'm going stir-crazy in here? What I need is to be outside beneath the big blue Texas sky, and I'll be fine."

"I know you will be." Tenderness gathered behind his sternum, but surely it wasn't tenderness, it only felt that way. It had to be worry for what the kids had gone through, seeing her fall off her horse, expecting her to get up and praying for her to be fine but she wasn't. The rush to the hospital, the terror in the waiting room, the fear and anguish at her bedside praying for her to come back to them.

Thank You, Lord, he prayed automatically, as if caring about Belle was second nature. Once it had been. Now, she was the mother of their children, nothing more. It made him sad. He waited while she tapped away at the phone she drew from her pocket, her auburn hair tumbling forward to curtain her face. When she was done he tucked the chairs into place beneath the table and waited for her to amble into the aisle.

"I know the girls were planning to keep me company for lunch anyway," Belle explained. "I told her to bring the boys along. We'll tell them over the meal."

"I know that look." The furrow across her forehead. "You're worried about how they are going to take this."

"I've spent twenty-five years second-guessing my decision." She halted, her pearled teeth digging into her lush bottom lip. Vulnerability carved into her face, showing every bit of the gentle girl with the big heart he'd fallen in love with once. "Their safety wasn't the only reason I didn't tell them the truth. I was afraid they would hate me for separating us. For not letting you and the other half of the twins come with us."

"That wasn't your fault, Belle." It cut him in two to think back upon that unhappy time. "We both made that decision, remember? We agreed to stay apart. It was for the best."

"Yes, but will they understand?" For all her strength and bravado, Belle's world had revolved around her children. Clearly that was as true as it had ever been.

"We'll do our best to make them understand."

"Maybe now is a good time to tell you something else. The twins received Bibles from an anonymous person while I was in my coma. There were notes inside asking for forgiveness. There was no explanation and I can't help but wonder if it could be from him?"

"I'll find out. I promise you." He reached out to cover her hand, wanting to comfort her and reassure her, but hesitated. Maybe it wasn't a good idea.

As if she agreed, she gave his outstretched hand a worried look, straightened her shoulders and moved forward. "I think I need to lie down for a while."

"Fine." He stayed planted where he stood in

the corridor, watching her progress along the
tiled floor, hurrying away from him. Tall, lean,
graceful, even with a limp. It wasn't longing he
felt—his affection for Belle was in the past—
but he couldn't put his finger on what emotion
tugged at him. Perhaps he would always want
to make things better for Belle, always want to
make her happy.

Not that he'd ever been able to do so. Shoulders braced, he headed for the nurses' station. He
had a few questions for Belle's doctors.

"…Lord bless us and keep us. Amen." Belle
finished the blessing, trying to keep her voice
from wobbling with nerves. Thankful for her
faith that sustained her and for her family, united
and happy, she opened her eyes and gave Violet's
hand one last squeeze before releasing it.

For a minute it was like seeing double—two
identical sons and two identical daughters seated
in wicker chairs around a patio table watching
her every move. No doubt for signs of weakness. They worried over her health too much.
She was a Texas girl, born and bred. She was
tough, she was resilient and she'd defeat the last
effects of her head injury in no time. She hated
that they were troubled. Worse, she hated the
crinkle of concern carved into Brian's handsome
face. Movie-star handsome, she might add. Hon-

est piercing brown eyes, exquisite cheekbones and the strongly angled jaw that maturity had only improved.

Now, why exactly was she noticing? Probably because it was better than the difficult story she was about to tell. Anxiety fluttered in her stomach, making the appetizing meal Lupita had packed for them look like a very bad idea indeed. Her midsection rolled, and her hunger tanked. The secret had lived inside her for so many years. She'd avoided this moment for more than one reason, for more reasons than she'd admitted to Brian. What if telling the truth brought more pain?

"Do you want me to start, Belle?" Brian couldn't be kinder as he searched her face across the length of table. Behind him a Christmas garland slung across the doorway into the sunroom. "I'd like to."

"You didn't mention that earlier." Her words were light and meant that way, but she couldn't help feeling annoyed. It was her story to tell, she was the one who'd torn this family apart long ago. Hadn't that been how she'd spent the past hour in her room, practicing what she would say and how she would say it? Fearing all the while the twins wouldn't understand. That they would resent her for disrupting their childhoods and separating them for over two decades. Each twin had grown up alone because of her.

"If you want to go first, then go." Brian nodded absently, and Carter slipped a pulled pork sandwich onto his plate. Brian's entire focus zeroed in on her. "Let me take the blame."

"But you aren't at fault." His steadfast tone almost made her believe it.

"You weren't the one who saw—" She stopped herself, seeing it happen all over again.

"Mom, what's going on?" Jack leaned forward in his chair. "What did you see?"

"Yeah…what's this all about?" Grayson asked.

"Mom, you look upset." Violet took her hand again and squeezed.

"The doctor said you aren't supposed to be stressed." Maddie frowned, taking her other hand. "Dad, what's got her so worked up?"

Belle shook her head. See how the man made her crazy? He'd always stirred her up, messed with her normally logical mind and turned everything on end. It wasn't that they were arguing, exactly. She laughed at herself. Some things never changed. "Fine, Brian, you go first."

Across the table, the man arched one brow as if to ask if she was sure. She nodded, nerves prickling. This looked important to him. She wanted to be the one to tell the truth, the truth her children had been asking about for a long time. Brian hadn't been there, he hadn't been involved, but she wanted peace between them. Leave the arguments and the fighting in the past where it belonged. As if he could see all that in her eyes, he drew in a breath, straightened his spine and looked around the table at each child, now an adult, the sadness in his gaze strong enough to dilute the shining sun.

"Twenty-five years ago your mother and I divorced. We'd married young while we were still in high school, and this may come as a shock to you but we had to get married. That was my fault, and mine alone. This was before both Belle and I were Christians."

Brian's sincerity rumbled in deep, low notes. "I won't lie to you, it was tough being married that young. We had school to finish, and then your mother chose to drop out when the boys were born. That wasn't an easy sacrifice. I almost did, too, because juggling full-time work was too much, but your mother encouraged me to hang in there."

"You had dreams, Brian." It hurt to remember the young man he'd been, the integrity that had always been a part of him. Insisting he had to marry her, struggling as hard as he knew how to be a good husband to her and a proud father. Why did it hurt to remember the good as much as it did the bad? "You'd always wanted to be a doctor since you were a little boy."

"Yes, but I didn't want it to cost me my other dreams." He swallowed hard, telling her something she'd never guessed. Maybe being a father and a husband had been dreams of his, too.

And not something he'd been forced into. Tears burned behind her eyes and she blinked hard, refusing to let them fall, refusing to let him see.

"But it was too much. We couldn't make our marriage work. I'm sorry." Brian's baritone dipped. "Your mother and I tried as hard as we knew how. We both gave it everything we had. Everything."

"We did." The wrenching fights, the tears after, the knowledge that they were failing at the single most important job in their lives—as married parents of their beloved double set of twins. Stubborn tears filled her eyes, but she held Brian's gaze through the blur of them. No way could she let him take the sole blame for this. "I was the one who asked you to leave, Brian. I was the one who quit on you. I just couldn't take you so unhappy, and then it happened."

"I know." Although he was at the other end of the table, his compassion bridged the distance between them. "I thought the same thing. I always figured we'd find our way back to each other and then—"

"The Witness Protection Program." The words tumbled off her tongue. "If I hadn't left the doctor's office at that exact moment, then we never would have left."

"It's not your fault, Belle. It's the way things happened, that's all." Brian sounded as if he had no doubt. "I never blamed you for that. I admired you for having the strength and the guts to testify."

"You d-did?" She hated how her voice wobbled, betraying her. Lord help her, because Brian's opinion of her still mattered. She hadn't realized how much.

"Uh, Mom," Jack spoke, surprising her. She blinked, realizing she'd forgotten she and Brian were not alone, that they were being watched like leads in a Broadway play, their audience enthralled. "Did you say the *Witness Protection Program?*"

"Yes." The words felt torn out of her. "That's why we left your father, Maddie and Grayson behind. The three of us were taken into protective custody. We were never meant to meet again."

Chapter Four

"You mean we were in witness protection all this time?"

"But why?"

"How did that happen?"

"Why didn't you tell us?"

The questions erupted all at once, echoing around the sunroom and bouncing off the glass ceiling, but the regal and lovely woman across the table held his attention like no other. Belle sat tall and strong, folded her slim hands and let the questions roll over her. Gratitude shone quietly in the dark depths of her unguarded eyes. For an instant he saw both the woman he'd loved—the young Isabella full of life and spirit—and this newer Belle, seasoned and confident. Both intrigued him. Both touched him.

"We were sworn not to tell." He spoke above

the chaos of questions from their children, his gaze never wavering from Belle's.

The twins fell silent, although the room echoed with their frustrations and curiosity.

"It was the only way," he assured them. "Your mother witnessed a murder. She had Violet in her arms and Jack in a stroller. They were all in terrible danger. The thought of anything happening to you two—"

He stopped before his voice could break and betray him, his walls went up and he shut down the emotion before it surfaced. Just like he always did, he realized. Force of habit and one habit he had to break.

He gritted his teeth, took down his defenses and felt the terror of that long-ago time. "All I could think about was that man or his fellow drug dealers coming to gun you down, little Laurel and Tanner and my Isabella."

"Dad, that had to have been horrible to go through." Grayson patted him on the shoulder, the beloved son he'd had the privilege to raise. "Not knowing if they would ever be safe."

"That's why I testified." Belle appeared a little shell-shocked, perhaps she'd realized what he'd tried to tell her. Although they were divorced, at that time, he'd still thought of her as his Isabella. "Witness protection meant safety."

"But what happened exactly?" Violet wanted to know.

"You and Jack had awful earaches—I'd been up all night walking the floor with both of you," Belle answered. "Our pediatrician squeezed you into her schedule, and I was on my way to the car when I heard the shot. I turned toward the sound and there he was standing in the alley with a dead man at his feet."

"You had to be terrified, Mom." Maddie took her hand.

"Petrified. Literally, since I couldn't move. For an instant, I couldn't believe what I saw. I just stared at the man, the murderer. It was like something out of someone else's life." Belle's gentle face twisted with agony. "Then he pointed the gun at me."

"He tried to shoot you?" Jack bit out.

"He aimed, and all I could think about were my precious babies. I had to keep you safe." Conviction rang in her soft voice. "I got us away from there as fast as I could, although how was a mystery. I shook so hard, I could hardly run. I dashed back into the doctor's office, fearing all the while the murderer would follow us in and finish the job. That fear haunted me until the police arrived."

"And from there it happened so fast." Brian took over the story. "The marshals whisked the three of you away…we hardly had time to really say goodbye."

"There were a lot of things I meant to say and couldn't," Belle confessed, as if they were the only two in the room. "I'm so sorry, Brian. I hope you know—"

"I know." Solemn, understanding, the low notes in his words held the ring of truth. "It was a long time ago. We just weren't meant to be."

"Exactly." It was a hard truth to face. A lifetime separated her from Brian. Their divorce was so very long ago, making them both different people now.

"I don't understand." Violet spoke up, ripping Belle out of her thoughts. She realized all five children watched her breathlessly.

"It's a lot of information all at once." Her palms went damp and she gave a little push away from the table. Why was she trembling? Because the whole truth wasn't out there. She'd kept a piece of it back. Not wanting to talk about it, she gestured toward the food. "No one's eating. Lupita's feelings will be hurt. You know the pride she takes in her cooking."

"So this was what you were keeping from us all along?" Jack's handsome face compressed into hard lines. "Every time I asked about our father. Every time you refused. You could have told us the truth. All you had to do was to say we were in the Witness Protection Program."

"You could have told us, Dad." Maddie's gentle chiding felt like the first tumble of an avalanche before it crashed down a mountain and destroyed everything.

What if the twins couldn't understand? Belle worried. What if they blamed her?

They wouldn't be wrong to do so. She steeled her spine, determined to face the consequences of her long-ago decisions. Consequences she knew would hurt if they ever came to light.

"Yeah, Dad, at least we would have known," Grayson chimed in. "You let us believe Sharla was our real mother."

"You were so young, too young to understand, don't you see?" Brian stood up, towering above them. His dark hair tumbled over his forehead as he surveyed each child. "It was hard for me to look at you every day and realize your twin was out there somewhere in the world and not knowing where. I wanted to tell you, but Violet and Jack were witnesses, too, and safer with your mother if nobody knew. It was a decision we made out of love, you have to understand that."

Thank you. Belle thought the words, and although she didn't say them, she knew Brian heard them.

"We get it." Jack spoke first. "But we aren't

children anymore, Mom. You could have told me all about this. Or do you think I wouldn't have understood?"

"I was afraid you would try to find your father and your twin." She squeezed Maddie's hand and then Violet's. Did the girls know how much she loved them? "I couldn't risk your safety. When we moved back to Texas from Washington State, I figured we were all right as long as we kept the past buried."

"But I unearthed it," Maddie chimed in. "And I'm not sorry we found each other, Violet."

"Me, either," Violet seconded, sharing a look with her twin.

It did Belle's heart good to see the girls together. And the boys—so responsible and capable and, when she glanced at Jack's face, so gloomy. Yes, it was time to be fully honest. "In truth, I feared you might blame me for taking you away."

"It wasn't your fault," Carter spoke up. She loved that boy, too. She'd only known him a short time, but he'd already made a lasting impression on her heart. In many ways, he reminded her so much of his father. "You did what you had to do. Sometimes that's the way life is. You made the best of a bad situation. You moved away from Dad. You kept everyone safe. It couldn't have been easy to leave your kids behind."

Yes, she definitely loved that boy. "It killed me. I'm so sorry, Maddie. Grayson. Having to leave you was the hardest thing I'd ever done."

"Why didn't you take us with you?" A muscle jumped along Grayson's jawline. "You could have done it. You took two kids into witness protection. Two more wouldn't have been difficult."

"Yes, Mom. Why did you go without us?" A flash of pain misted Maddie's eyes.

Belle's undoing. Tears rose in a burning lump in her throat, and she couldn't speak. She couldn't answer because how could they understand? What if they turned away from her? What if she lost them again? She didn't think she could take it.

"She left you behind because I loved you both so much," Brian answered. "When our marriage failed, your mother knew how devastated I was, because she was just as devastated. I'd lost too much. I couldn't bear to lose all of my children, as well. Your mother suggested this solution." He breathed deeply. "That's Belle, that's who she is. You don't blame her. If you have to be angry at someone, then you're angry at me. Got it?"

"We got it, Dad." Grayson's answer resonated low and deep.

"Yes, Dad," Maddie answered.

"No wonder you were always so sad, Mom." Violet's grip tightened around her fingers. "You tried to hide it, but sometimes at night when I'd get up to get a drink of water, I'd see you sitting alone in the shadows."

"I hate it if I made it harder for you, Mom." Jack's apology sounded torn from him. "I wish I'd known. I never would have argued with you, you never would have fallen off the horse—"

"I should have trusted you with the truth, both of you." She could see that now. "It was too dangerous, and it hurt too much to look at what I'd lost. Going forward and keeping the past where it belonged was safer."

"And now look where that has brought us." Brian's words snared her attention. "Together again. Your mother's right. Lupita went to a lot of trouble to pack this lunch, so we'd better enjoy it. Eat up. Don't worry…everything is going to be all right. I'll make sure of it."

The surge of gratitude rippled through her. Brian was a man of his word, she knew. He'd do his best to make sure their children were safe. Somewhere out there was David Johnson, the man who'd threatened her in the courtroom, the man who had mercilessly committed murder in cold blood and could have killed Belle and maybe Jack and Violet, too.

Wherever he is, keep him away from my children, Lord, please. No matter what, keep them safe. She sent the silent prayer heavenward as the conversation turned to the latest news at the ranch—apparently the hired hand Emmett Potter and Lupita's niece Carolyn were still dating. Belle smiled, glad to still be in the loop with things at home. After telling the truth, her children were still here, lovingly gathered around her and in no small part due to Brian. She owed him for that. Huge. Big-time. He really had grown into the man she'd always known he would be.

"Thanks, Doctor." Brian glanced over his shoulder down the hall of Ranchland Manor, distracted by the echo of laughter from Belle's room. Sounded like the kids were having a good time saying their goodbyes. He turned his attention back to Belle's doctor. "I appreciate your time."

"No problem. I'll take your recommendation into consideration." Doc Garth flipped through Belle's chart. "I can't say I haven't been tempted. She's one of the most motivated patients I've seen."

"That's Belle." Wistfulness ached in his chest. The two of them weren't meant to be—he knew that—but he respected her. He wanted to help her. "She may recover more completely at home. It's not as if she's lacking in people to care for her there."

"No, I've noticed that. Two sets of twins. They

create quite a sensation wherever they go." Garth grinned. "The first time I saw them, I thought I was seeing double."

"They have that effect on people." Brian shook the man's hand. "Thanks for the update. I can see Belle's getting great care."

"We try. Hey, my clinic next door could use another physician. I know you've got a practice up in Fort Worth, but it's something to keep in mind should circumstances change."

"I don't see how they would, but thanks." Brian appreciated it. As he headed down the hall, he wondered what Belle would think if he moved to Grasslands. Pretty sure that wouldn't go over well. Not at all. Besides, he was settled in Fort Worth. The twins wouldn't want their old man hanging around, would they?

"Hey, Dad." Carter ambled into sight. "We're getting ready to go. I've got errands to run and then I'm going to check in on Savannah. Want to come along?"

"You go on. I'll see you back at the ranch." He strolled down the corridor, every step bringing him closer to Belle. There were things he needed to tell her that could only be said in private. He hugged his youngest, listening to the goodbyes ringing in the room behind him. Sounded like Grayson and Jack were discussing the house Grayson was renovating in town. Apparently

Gray could hardly wait to move in there with his fiancée, Elise, and her little boy after they were married. While the guys droned on about drywall and state-of-the-art appliances, the girls entertained themselves by making Christmas shopping plans.

Christmas. Hard to believe it was that time of year already. He'd never been more grateful as he stepped through the door.

"Don't think you're going to get out of it that easy, Mom." Violet shook her head. "Honestly, all we've been hearing is how you don't need to slow down."

"One mention of the mall and she suddenly needs to take it easy." Maddie's laughing eyes said it all. She was grateful to have her mother back after all these years. "Wasn't someone going stir-crazy in here?"

"Stir-crazy for the *ranch*," Belle corrected with a laugh as she settled into an armchair. "Not the mall. If someone would bring my laptop from home, I could do all my shopping with a few clicks."

"Are you sure she's my mother?" Maddie teased gently, bending down to kiss Belle's cheek. "Let's put it this way. You don't have a choice, lady. When you least expect it, Violet and I are going to drag you away to the land of the department stores."

"I guess this means you really aren't mad at me?" Belle searched her daughter's face. "All those years you grew up without a mother or Violet. You don't resent it, even a little bit?"

"I wish you had never witnessed that murder, Mom. I wish the whole thing hadn't happened at all. I'm mad at the murderer, I'm mad we lost years together, but learning that I had a mom again after losing Sharla was the best news I could have." Maddie swiped her eyes. "I agree with Dad. Everything is all right now. We go on from here as a family."

"Exactly." Violet kissed Belle's cheek. "If you need anything, text or call. I'll come running."

"And I'll send you an update on the cattle you were asking about." Grayson donned his Stetson, ready to help on the ranch while he was here. He still worked in Fort Worth—where his fiancée and her young son resided—but would be moving to Grasslands when his new job started at month's end. "Your horse misses you. I'll take her out for a run this afternoon and get her a little exercise."

"I miss Mouse, my girl, but not for much longer. I intend to get on that horse as soon as I'm sprung from this place." Belle's comment surprised no one, and especially not Brian. During their marriage, she'd been headstrong and tenacious. Looked like that hadn't changed, either.

A less intrepid or gutsy woman might not want to hop back up on her horse first thing after the devastating accident that had left her in a coma.

"Don't even tell me that." Jack shook his head. "What does the doctor say?"

"No idea." Belle's confidence shone like polished amber as her gaze met his. "Where are you off to, Brian?"

"Thought I'd hang around for a few minutes. Unless you're going to kick me out, too?"

"Tempting, but you may as well stay. We have business to discuss."

"We do." He held up his phone to confirm it.

"Then we'll see you at the ranch, Dad." Grayson gripped his shoulder on the way by. "If you make it back in time, I'll take you riding."

"Me, on a horse?" He shook his head. "Sorry, that's not likely. But I would like a tour of the ranch. It's an impressive place."

"Will do." Jack turned on his boot heel and followed his twin out the door.

"Mom, don't be too hard on Dad," Violet said from the hallway. "We just got him back. We don't want you to scare him off."

"I have a knack for scaring off things," Belle agreed. "Varmints, coyotes and even an ex-husband on occasion."

"Exactly how many ex-husbands do you have?"

he quipped, although he knew he was her one and only. "I'd better be careful around you."

"Yes, sir." She glanced at the doorway, now empty, all signs of their children gone. "What exactly are you doing on my ranch?"

"It's where I spent last night."

"Excuse me? You used my ranch house as a bed-and-breakfast?" She wasn't sure she liked that, not at all. "Was the hotel in town booked?"

"No idea. When I heard you were here in Grasslands, I just came. I barely packed a change of clothes." He felt weary, hating he wasn't up to par from his illness. He eased onto the soft cushion of the other armchair and faced her. "And when I discovered you'd been hurt, figuring out where I would spend the night was the last thing on my mind."

"So the kids put you up at the ranch. It must be pretty crowded there."

"Yes, ma'am. It's a big house, but every bed was taken. I bunked on the sofa in the den."

"Brian, that's hardly comfortable. You're recovering, too." Concern rushed through her. Fine, she couldn't help it. "One of the boys should have given you his room."

"The couch is just fine. I'm used to much worse these days. Trust me."

"That's right. The kids told me you do a lot of missionary work, doctoring the poorest of the poor." Admiration mixed with the concern, a lethal combination. There was so much about Brian to like. "I always knew you would make a difference as a doctor. When the kids told me you'd gone to medical school, just like we'd always hoped for, I couldn't have been, well, more proud."

"Is that so? A few moments ago, I was sure you were mad as a hornet at me for hanging out at your ranch."

"Not as mad as a hornet," she corrected. "Irked. I just learned you are back and here you are, everywhere. Roaming through the halls of Ranchland Manor, hanging around my room and now sleeping in my house. I'm not ready for that."

"I know exactly what you mean. All these years apart without so much as a whisper from you, and now you're front and center. And our kids." He stopped, shook his head, met her gaze. "They turned out well. You raised them up right. They are great human beings."

"I can say the same about you, Brian. Maddie is a doll, Grayson is just like you, and Carter— there just aren't words." She knew her affection showed. "Isn't it amazing how alike they are after being apart nearly all of their lives?"

"I know. I have to do a double take to make sure Maddie is Maddie."

"And that Jack is Jack." The issues between them faded and suddenly they were laughing. "Remember when the girls were just wee things and you put the wrong clothes on Maddie?"

"Pink and green. That's how we told them apart." Brian nodded, lost in the memory, too. "It was all my fault, I was trying to give you some downtime and bathe the twins."

"I wound up coloring with the boys." Belle recalled those good, sweet times. How happy the house had been when there was a lull in their fighting and the weight of their financial worries. The moment had been serene. "Suddenly I hear this 'uh-oh' from our bedroom."

"I'd put pink on one twin, but I wasn't sure I had the right twin. As the other one was fresh from her bath, I had no way to be sure." Brian shook his head, scattering his thick dark hair. The love shining in his eyes, mixed with humor, warmed her heart. "I couldn't tell them apart."

"Remember how panicked you were? Poor Brian."

"I was afraid Maddie was really Violet—or Laurel, as she was named then—and they'd spend the rest of their lives mixed up. You came to the rescue."

"I could always tell them apart." She laughed softly, remembering barreling into the nursery to see Brian with his hands to his head, more than a little stressed. "We got Maddie in pink and Violet, well, Laurel, in green and all was right with the world."

"We did have some good moments." His eyes sparkled, as if he recalled what happened after both sets of twins were down for the night.

They'd broken into the stash of bottled root beer, a treat since their very small budget was stretched tight, and settled down together on the couch. One of her favorite old movies was on, and they cuddled, sharing little comments, quiet laughter, and stealing kisses as the movie played out to a happy ending.

A happy ending was what she'd wanted more than life then.

"Good moments? Yes, we had a few," she agreed. How sweet they'd been. "We got four beautiful children out of the deal. And Carter."

"Yes, we did." Brian's smile lit up his face, gave her a glimpse of the good-hearted boy he used to be. The boy she'd loved so much.

"Thanks for sticking by me today." She wished she didn't feel so close to Brian. "What you said to the kids made a difference. They aren't mad at me, when they have the right to be."

"No, I'm the one to blame. That's the truth, and God knows it." Brian's smile faded. The light in his deep eyes dimmed. "I wasn't the best husband. I should have tried harder. I should have listened better. Then maybe we could have made it work."

"That's not true." She'd tried as hard as she'd known how at the time. So had Brian. "Remember the way we drove each other crazy? Babies crying with colic on top of teething, toddlers with diapers to be changed and earaches along with bills and that impossible budget we were on. I was stuck home, while you were constantly working or studying. The rare time we spent together, we mostly argued. We were unhappy."

"I made you unhappy, Belle."

What they needed was a change of subject. "Did you hear from Tommy?" Hard as she tried to push it to the back of her mind, she was reminded yet again of the danger they still could be facing.

"He's tracked down the marshal responsible for your case. Old case, I should say." Brian pulled out his phone to squint at a text message. "He's out on assignment, but they're looking into it. He says if the murderer had been released, they would have been notified and passed that info along."

"At least David Johnson isn't running around at large." Belle stretched her slender legs out in front of her. "He would be middle-aged. It's been twenty-five years. That's too long to hold on to a vendetta, isn't it?"

"No idea. We don't know what he's thinking." Brian attempted to hide the twist of raw fear coursing through him. What would she think if she knew how he was feeling?

"A lot can change in twenty-five years. Look how much we have changed."

"I'm not sure about that. You haven't changed all that much." He really ought to try to suppress the warmth he felt. Nostalgia, probably, and respect for the woman she'd turned into. "I told your doctor not to expect you to sit around Ranchland Manor placidly doing your physical therapy. You'll push as hard as you can. My guess is you'll progress enough to be out of here by end of the week at the latest."

"You talked to my doctor?" Dark fire in her eyes blazed him as she sat up in her chair, facing him angrily. "You just decided to make my recovery your business?"

"Well, I wanted to help. You know how Jack feels about the accident." The warning alarm in his gut went off like a firehouse claxon. "I was trying to reassure him, that's all."

"Doing him a favor?" She arched one slim brow, her gaze so furious he was surprised it didn't leave scorch marks.

"I only meant to help, Belle." He held up both hands in a show of surrender. His instincts were shouting at him to retreat fast. "No need to get upset."

"I'm not upset."

"Well, good. That's a relief." He blew out a breath he hadn't realized he'd been holding. "You've been in a deep coma. You've incurred a serious head injury. I thought maybe I could—"

"You thought?" She eased up onto the edge of her cushion, a lioness ready to pounce. "You *thought?*"

Uh-oh. Looked like he'd messed up again. "Sorry, I just meant—"

"Perhaps it would be better if instead of thinking, next time you want to poke your nose in my business, you *ask* first."

"Ask. Right. I should have done that." Only, Jack had confided to him earlier and he'd spotted the doc and started making small talk—

"You could have asked me instead of going through my medical records. That's private, Brian, and you haven't been my husband in twenty-five years." Hurt shadowed her gaze as she launched out of her chair. Her hands quaked as she grabbed the walker's grip, betraying her emotions.

He knew Belle wasn't genuinely angry with him. She was hurting. Whatever talking to her doctor had done, it had stirred up issues he hadn't taken the time to discover. He sighed, praying for wisdom, then followed her across the room. "I'm sorry, Belle."

"I know. I didn't mean to get so upset." She couldn't meet his gaze as she searched through a stack of books on her bedside table. "You'll let me know what else Tommy finds out?"

"You'll be the first to know." He hesitated, wanting to lay his hand on the nape of her neck the way he had when they'd been married, willing comfort through his touch. He'd disappointed her again, and that disappointment served as a reminder of every way he'd let her down in the past.

It looked like he still had the gift for it, so he headed for the door. "I'll be in touch, Belle."

"See ya, Brian." She took her Bible from the stack and clutched it to her chest like a lifeline. "Bye."

Her message was clear. He turned on his heel and kept on walking. She was no longer his Isabella, but remembering how he'd once loved her softened a part of his heart that had grown hard and cold over the years.

Chapter Five

"Dad, you wanted to see me?" Grayson strode into the den of the Colbys' impressive ranch house. "So, from the looks of it, you aren't leaving?"

"Lupita offered to do some of my laundry. I couldn't say no." It was the truth, but he also dodged the fact that he was leaving his duffel packed. He knew Belle wasn't exactly thrilled he was staying in her home. He tossed a T-shirt into the laundry basket on the floor. "Look at you. Ranch life agrees with you."

"Can't deny it. I like helping Jack out. It brings us closer. I love it here." Grayson jabbed his hands into his jean pockets. "Of course knowing I'll soon be moving here permanently with Elise and her son might have something to do with that."

"I'm glad you've found a good woman to

love." He'd had a lot of news to digest over the past twenty-four hours. He still couldn't believe that while he'd been gone, every one of his children had fallen in love. Suddenly the Wallace family had grown by leaps and bounds. He looked forward to the excitement of weddings and grandchildren to come. "What is the boy's name again?"

"Cory. He's six. He's awesome." Grayson's face softened and his voice warmed, telling Brian everything he needed to know. "I want you to meet him and Elise."

"That's just what I was going to suggest. If you love them, then I do."

"Thanks, Dad. That means a lot." Grayson swallowed hard, a question shadowed in his eyes, one that remained unasked. Brian wanted to know what was going on, but first things first.

"I was hoping you would tell me about the note and Bible your mother mentioned to me." He tossed a pair of jeans into the basket, zipped his duffel and straightened up. "She said it was anonymous."

"I have no idea who sent it, and believe me I did my investigative work. I still couldn't figure it out." Grayson had the cool strength of a cop and the thoroughness of a detective. "I guess our family meeting today answered a few questions I've had. Mainly why Belle Colby didn't exist until twenty-five years ago and why Isabella Wallace disappeared all those years ago."

"You really did your research." He ran a hand through his hair.

"We had to. You weren't here to answer our questions, and Belle wasn't able to." Grayson headed over to the window and gazed out at the wide Texas sky. Cirrus clouds trailed in front of the sun, casting the expansive ranch in shadow. "Witness protection. That never entered my mind. Is it safe for all of this to come to light?"

"That's what I need to find out." Brian thought of Belle and the ordeal she'd been through. "Your mother has been hiding long enough. Do you think the letters are a clue?"

"I do. We all got them, even Carter. That's why we thought the sender might be you."

"Me?" Brian followed his son into the hallway. Tall ceilings led the way toward the rise of staircase and past the kitchen toward the front part of the house. He caught a glimpse of Jack speaking with the housekeeper. Wearing a Stetson, the boy had clearly just come in from the barns.

"That's why we told Belle when she first woke up." Grayson took the stairs two at a time. "We thought you were apologizing for breaking up the family."

"And after what we learned from Patty Earl,"

Jack piped in, heading toward the living room, "we had a lot of reason to suspect you."

"Patty Earl?" Brian's feet felt rooted to the floor. None of this was making sense. "What does she have to do with this? I haven't heard that name in a long time."

"Maybe since the boys were born?" Maddie and Violet asked as they passed Grayson on the staircase, heading closer. It really was something to see them together, identical smiles, bouncing auburn hair, eyes just like their mother's. Both wore yellow—Maddie a fashionable blouse and Violet a henley—along with their jeans.

"Jack, I'm not sure this is the time…" Violet said, giving her ponytail a flip.

"There's no time like the present," Jack argued. "Besides, you know we haven't been able to bring this up with Mom. She's fragile right now."

"She's stronger than you think." Violet swirled around the newel post and into the family room. "But we don't want to do anything to interrupt her recovery."

"Especially when she is doing so well," Maddie agreed, tucking a sleek lock of hair behind one ear.

"I feel like the outsider," Brian quipped. "What has been going on?"

"Grayson is bringing down his letter. You'll

see." Maddie took Brian's hand and led him toward the leather couch. "One thing at a time. Tell us that you agree with Mom's doctor's course of treatment."

"It's standard protocol in cases like this." He eased onto the cushion, more tired than he'd realized. Getting weight off his feet felt good. He smiled in thanks as Lupita appeared with a tray of steaming tea. He took a cup and sipped, letting the warmth sustain him. Just what he needed.

"It's hard seeing Mom struggling to walk." Violet plopped down next to him. "They say it may be temporary, but we worry. What if it's not? What can we do to help her? Mom is active and vital and it'll kill her if she can't get back to who she used to be."

"Prayer helps."

"We've been doing that." Jack eased down on the couch, turning to face his father. "A lot of it. I keep thinking we need to get her a top specialist from Fort Worth or Dallas. Would that help?"

"Not that I can see. She's in good hands, and her progress is remarkable." With Belle, he'd expect nothing less. His chest tightened painfully thinking of how they'd left things. "If she keeps it up, she'll be back on her feet before we know it."

"I'm glad you're here." Violet smiled. "For a lot of reasons, but it's nice to have a dad."

"It's good to be your dad." Pride filled him as he gazed upon his children. This was an answered prayer.

"Here it is, Dad." Grayson crossed the room, holding out a Bible. "We all received them. The same Bible, the same note."

"Let me take a look." Brian set down his cup and flipped through the Good Book. He found the handwritten note and read it carefully.

I am sorry for what I did to you and your family. I hope you and your siblings, especially your twin, can forgive me as I ask the Lord to forgive me.

He stared at the words, words that he knew in his gut had to come from the murderer, from the man who had torn apart the Wallace family.

Forgiveness. Could he do it? He clamped his molars together, remembering the man who'd stood up and disrupted court, threatening Belle. David Johnson was the reason Brian hadn't been able to see Jack and Violet since they were small. David Johnson was the reason Belle was wrenched out of Brian's life permanently and all possibility of reconciliation between them ended.

"If this isn't from you, then could it be from the murderer Mom testified against?" Grayson asked.

"That makes sense." Brian nodded. "I have a call in to the marshal who handled your mother's case, the man responsible for keeping her, Violet and Jack safe. I'll let him know about this."

"If the notes are from David Johnson, then we have our answer for that. At least that's another mystery almost solved, and we may no longer be in jeopardy." Jack blew out a sigh of relief, looking as if he had more to say, but Grayson, Maddie and Violet all shook their heads at him.

Brian was tempted to ask what was going on when Grayson stood.

"Let's find a football game." He headed out of the room. The TV was in the den. "We can all watch. Spend some quality time together."

"Sounds good. Violet, maybe you could ask Lupita to put out snacks for us," Jack suggested, getting to his feet. "You girls can join us if you want. We'll make an afternoon of it."

"Great, I'll give Lupita a hand." Maddie popped up and headed toward the kitchen. "Chips and dips, popcorn, peanuts. Does that sound good with y'all?"

"It sounds great, darlin'." Brian had never seen Maddie so happy. Love looked good on her, too. He had yet to meet the ranch foreman who'd captured his daughter's heart, but he was looking forward to it.

"I'll help." Violet ambled after her, just as happy and in love as her sister. Last summer, she'd fallen for Landon Derringer, a wealthy businessman who used to be sweet on Maddie.

"It's good to have you here, Dad." Grayson settled down on the couch in the den and patted the empty cushion beside him. "Like old times, you and me watching the game."

"No, not just old times." Brian's throat tightened, looking around from one son to the other. "This is the way it was meant to be. All of us together."

He watched as Jack grabbed the remote and found a Texas team and the group of them turned toward the screen, cheering for a Longhorns victory. If only Belle were home and healed and out of harm's way. Thinking of his ex-wife, his mind filled with painful emotions he didn't want to name. He prayed they would all be safe from David Johnson.

What was Brian doing right now? Belle wondered as she searched through the box for another edge piece. The ladies had started another jumbo jigsaw puzzle in the common room. The day had been pleasant, but she missed her ranch. She longed to be out on the open range riding Mouse, or in the house getting down the Christmas ornaments with Violet. The first Saturday in December was the afternoon they'd always put up the Christmas tree.

Did Brian keep up that tradition, too?

"Yoo-hoo." Marjorie broke through Belle's thoughts. "You have the piece I need."

"Sorry." She absently set the cardboard edge on the table and scooted it in the older woman's direction. "I don't know where my mind is."

"Tell me about it." Eunice chuckled, studying the pieces in front of her carefully with her bifocals. "It was all the starch with supper. Give me pasta and I'm in a happy state the rest of the evening."

"You and me both," Anna agreed.

It wasn't a carb overload, not in her case. She knew the cause beyond all doubt. Brian stayed on her mind. She couldn't forget the look on his face when she'd scolded him for helping himself to her medical records. His shock and the crinkle of unhappiness etched across his forehead as he apologized got to her. She'd felt the weight of his remorse as surely as if it had been her own.

In all honesty, her anger toward him hadn't been genuine. Something else had been going on. He'd threatened to draw her heart to his, something that could never happen again. This wasn't the past, they were no longer married, he was not her soul mate.

She sorted through the puzzle box, scanning for more edge pieces. Strange how after all this time, talking with Brian still felt second nature.

With him, both her words and her emotions came easily to the surface, just the way they always had. No man, not one in all the years since, had come close to making her feel that way.

The question was why. Why did she still feel akin to him? She tried to keep her mind on the puzzle, but Marjorie tugged the box from her.

"Goodness, let me do that. You are a million miles away, dear."

"I guess I am." She chuckled at herself. Look at her, daydreaming about Brian. What about him? Was he wondering how insane it was to have gotten so close, for just a moment? Nothing had changed. They still fought, she still got mad at him—but the truth was, she hadn't been mad as much as agitated over the thought that he might care for her, just a little bit.

Her heart lurched to a stop as she rose from the chair, and she thumped away from the table. She answered her friends who called out after her, hardly aware of what she said to them. Something pleasant, some promise to come back and help with the puzzle later, but really, she couldn't be sure. Mostly because she was too busy wrestling with the realization that she still cared for him.

"Belle!" One of the nurse's aides called across the hall to her. "Hel-lo! Earth to Belle. Your phone is ringing."

"I wondered what that jingling sound was," Belle quipped, stopping to tug her cell from her pocket and squint at the screen. Guess who. "Hi, Brian?"

"Hey, stranger." His wonderful, chocolate-smooth voice filled her ear. The way her heart jumped again was a sure sign that something was wrong.

Not wrong, she realized. No, that was too mild a word. This was a total catastrophe. The realization felt too new, something she needed time to process. How was she going to handle it? She cleared her throat, praying for the strength to play this cool. "It seems I owe you an apology."

"You do? Not that I recall."

Why did he have to be so gallant? She'd totally overreacted, but he didn't seem the least bit upset at how she'd treated him. He was awesome, so no wonder she'd been so volatile with these unwanted emotions lurking within. She tucked the phone against her shoulder and took a careful step forward. "I got a little testy with you today."

"I deserved it. I overstepped my boundaries. You reminded me I needed to respect them. Caring for you comes naturally, Belle. I trust you'll set me straight the next time I do it."

"I'm up for that job." Was she smiling again? What had happened to playing it cool? "So, what's going on?"

"Grayson and I did a little research tonight." In the background a warning chime clanged away and silenced. What sounded like a car door being shut. "I found out what happened to David Johnson."

"You did? Bless you, Brian." The long-standing worry in her stomach clutched into a hard ball. Whatever the news was, she would handle it.

Please don't let him be out of jail with revenge in his heart, she prayed.

The wind whooshing across the connection made her curious. "Where exactly are you?"

"About five steps from your front door."

"The news can't be good if you're delivering it in person." Was that her pulse thudding in her ears? She could hardly hear his answer.

"Trust me, this news is not what you are expecting."

Brian didn't seem as if he was overly concerned. No stress tightened his voice, and that had to mean they weren't dealing with the worst-case scenario. Her head shot up and there he was striding around the corner, stalwart and true, looking manly in a button-down shirt and blue jeans. She didn't notice the noise of her walker or her maddeningly slow gait as the deep notes of his voice warmed the air.

"Look at you go, Belle. I can't believe the progress you're making."

She didn't dare let his warmth affect her. She kept those barricades up, cool as a clam. "I should hope my walk is improving. I've been practicing all afternoon."

"All afternoon? That doesn't surprise me. No one but you, Belle." His voice smiled.

She forced herself to glance away from the smile carving into his face. Truth was, she had a soft spot for Brian's grin. "I'm determined to get out of here soon."

"Yes, your doc mentioned that to me." He turned and gestured toward the front lobby. "Are you up for a temporary escape?"

"Are you kidding? I get to leave this place?"

"For an hour. I already got permission from Doc Garth." He adjusted his gait to match hers. "And before you get bent up again, I thought you would want to get out of here."

"I should get bent up again, but I'm grateful."

"Good. Then let's go." He stopped at the desk and smiled absently at the receptionist. The receptionist blushed as he scribbled on a clipboard, unaware of the effect he had on most women.

But not her. No way, no how. Belle headed toward the sliding doors and hated that now she was lying to herself. She hadn't meant to. She wanted it to be true. She didn't want to respond in the slightest when Brian turned his intense gaze on her and his mouth hooked up in the corners.

But instead of coming close to her, say sliding his palm against the small of her back to guide her, as he would have done when they were married, he kept a polite distance between them.

Whatever the moment of closeness they'd shared earlier, it was gone. He was deliberately making it so.

Good decision, she thought. *That's my vote, too.* It was just what she wanted as he opened his car door for her. He kept a respectful space between them as she settled onto the front seat. Space was exactly what she wanted.

So why the twist of disappointment? She should be relieved.

Brian shut her door and strode out of sight. She tried not to monitor his progress in the side-view mirror, firmly willing her eyes to whatever was in front of her. It was easier to look at the glint of the parking-lot lights on the windshield, the bulking shadow of Ranchland Manor and the hint of stars sparkling across the black velvet of the Texas sky.

Brian's door opened and he folded his big frame behind the wheel. "You look happy to be out of that place."

"Ecstatic." There were her emotions on the

surface again. She buckled in, feeling awkward, wishing she knew how to navigate these uncertain waters. How did one act toward her former husband, especially when she apparently still had feelings for him?

"After seeing where you live, I get it." Brian started the car and backed out of the space. "You own an amazing piece of the Texas landscape. Jack promised me a tour after church tomorrow. I'm looking forward to learning about Colby Ranch."

"We run cattle, but Jack will tell you all about that." Why was she babbling? Probably to fill up the space between them with easy words, ones that wouldn't reveal too much. "Are they making you comfortable at the house?"

"It feels like home. You've done a wonderful job, Belle. A stranger can walk through the door and feel like they've always belonged."

"I'm glad. It's good you're staying there. I shouldn't have been mad about that earlier. That way you can get closer to Violet and Jack."

"I have all the time in the world for that." Kind, incredibly kind, Brian steered them out of the parking lot and down a dark street. The quiet joy etched on his features said everything.

"The kids want to get to know you, too. You mean just as much to them." She knew what he was feeling. She'd always been linked to this man.

"I keep thanking the Lord for bringing the twins together." He kept his gaze on the street, steering competently with one hand, and hit the blinker. "God must have had a hand in reuniting Violet and Maddie in the café that day. He wanted them to find each other."

"I have to believe it's because we are all finally safe."

"You are." Brian turned into a restaurant lot and aimed for the drive-through lane. "Tommy called me with the news. David Johnson died in prison six months ago."

Relief poured through her in an icy flood. She slumped against the seat, jaw dropped, trying to process. That meant the threat was over. The man couldn't hurt anyone. She should be rejoicing. She should be singing praises, but instead she felt oddly empty.

Brian started to reach for her, but the moment was broken when the drive-through attendant asked for their orders. "Two chocolate milk shakes," he said into the crackling speaker. Inside the restaurant a teenager asked if that would be all and gave a total. Brian drove to the window and handed over a few dollar bills. The cool evening air stung her face as she swallowed hard.

"Is it wrong to rejoice over someone else's death?" she asked softly.

"I know how you feel." Brian handed her a cold take-out cup, thanked the teen and pulled forward into an empty space near the front door. "That man cost both of us dearly. What we lost can't be measured. It can't be compensated for. I've never known terror until you told me that he'd pointed a gun at you while the man he'd killed lay at his feet."

"I've never hated him. I just—"

"Wished it could have been different?" Brian knew her thoughts. He always had, always would. Even with this careful distance between them. He didn't look at her. Instead he tore paper off one straw and handed it to her.

"Yes. I remember walking around the corner of the building and seeing the slain man slump to the ground." She willed her hand to stay steady as she took the straw and poked it through the opening in the plastic lid. "David Johnson looked up and I'll never forget how cold his eyes were. He simply raised his gun to me."

"It was grace that you moved before he could shoot."

"I remember a kick of superhuman adrenaline. I clutched Violet to me in her sling, turned Jack's stroller and ran. Their lives depended on it."

"Now it's really over," he said gruffly, staring deep into her eyes. "I feel the need to pray."

"You read my mind." She bowed her head, folded her hands and offered her gratitude to the Lord.

Chapter Six

"This was the perfect treat." Belle took a sip of her drink. "Thanks for thinking of it."

"My pleasure. Remember how you used to save up spare change to take you, Grayson and Jack out for milk shakes?" He leaned back in his seat, stirring his straw around in his cup.

"Some days I'd have to dig up every last penny from the bottom of my purse, from between the couch cushions."

"And every stray penny we came across in parking lots and on sidewalks."

"All to trade for chocolate milk shakes." Emotion stirred deep within her, an impossible something. She didn't want to examine the feeling too closely because she didn't want to fall for Brian again. She so, so didn't. "Remember the summer before the girls were born?"

"I could never forget. On the two evenings I had off during the week—"

"You worked two jobs," she remembered.

"—you would finish the supper dishes while I kept the boys entertained."

"And then we'd all walk down to the local drive-in together." That long-ago bliss filled her up, bringing with it the faint scent of roses from their neighbor's yard and the music of cicadas on the hot dry breeze. With the sun smiling down on them, they would walk hand in hand while Brian pulled the boys along in their red wagon. The wheels clunked over every line and crack in the sidewalk as the boys chattered and giggled. Her heart had brimmed with love.

"I can still see the wind dancing in your hair. You wore it longer then." Brian shifted in his seat. "Remember how the boys would have to stop and chase bugs and butterflies?"

"You were amazing with them." She did her best to keep the admiration from her tone, and was fairly sure she failed. "You would kneel down with them and watch the butterfly flit away. You are a good dad, Brian."

"Jack and Violet are all grown up. They may not need a dad the way they once did."

"Don't be too sure." She did her best not to notice the dependable line of Brian's shoulders or the bittersweet twist of his mouth. She wanted—no, she needed—to reassure him. "Jack and Violet have always wanted to know about you. Even after all these years, they never let it rest. Especially Jack."

"Jack is a fine man. You've raised him to be independent, strong, good. I only hope I can find a place in his life. In Violet's, too." He didn't look at her as he took a swallow of his icy, thick milk shake. "She's so like Maddie."

"I know what you mean." She nodded. "I look at her and it's as if I've always known her, as if those years lost don't truly matter. She's my daughter. Just as Grayson is my son. It's been so easy getting to know them. It will be the same for you. You'll see."

"I hope you're right." He blew out a breath. "Fort Worth isn't so far away that we can't meet up. I can drive here, I can invite them to my house for dinner."

"Wait a minute. Are you telling me that you cook?"

"I hired a housekeeper, but she taught me some basic skills. Enough to keep me from starving on her days off." A hint of humor, but he didn't turn toward her, share a smile and let her see the flash in his eyes.

"I'm sure the twins would love spending time with you." The words caught in her throat. Clearly she could see he wasn't interested in her. He didn't share the same new feelings she had for him. Why ever had she thought he could? A memory popped into her head, of the less-than-stellar times when they had been exhausted and disheartened. When there had been too many bills and not enough time together and she knew their marriage was failing. She shook her head. "Jack told me you watched a football game with them."

"Yep, we won by a field goal. A good game." He glanced at the dashboard clock. "Well, guess we'd better get you back."

"Right." So, that was it. He wasn't going to tell her about time spent with their children. He obviously didn't want to open up to her too much. What was wrong with her that she wanted him to?

"We should return a few minutes before our deadline." Brian put the car in gear. "I don't want to be late, because the kids want me to sign you out again tomorrow, too. For church."

"Tomorrow? Really?" Now, this was something she could be excited about. "You're going to spring me from the joint again?"

"The kids are." His subtle correction made her blush.

Okay, there was all the proof she needed. "Of course, that's what I meant. Now I'm really glad to have a doctor in the family."

"So far it's working out for you." A smile played along the edges of his mouth, although he stayed intent on his driving. He checked for traffic, backed out and steered toward the street. "The girls said something about stealing you away to church in the morning and afterwards talking wedding plans."

"Yes!" Belle punched the air. Things were good. She and Brian were negotiating this new relationship, she'd recovered enough for a day trip and the threat against her and the kids was over— Her mind reeled to a stop. "Hey, but one thing."

"Text the girls. Word is they are bringing an outfit for you for church." He turned into traffic and wheeled them down the street. "They seemed pretty sure how they intended to dress you."

"That isn't what occurred to me, but thanks." So, she liked the man, but she'd be smarter to focus on their current problems. "There's something I don't understand. The kids began receiving their Bibles recently. *After* David Johnson died. So—"

"He couldn't have sent them," Brian finished for her matter-of-factly. "It's impossible."

"That rules him out." Belle downed the last of her milk shake. "The question remains—"

"Who did?"

"I don't know." She felt awkward as silence

fell between them. "It makes sense Johnson may have come to regret his sins. But if he didn't—"

"Someone knows what happened to us and feels responsible." Brian steered into the parking lot and slid to a stop in a space near the front door. He twisted in his seat, facing her. "I wish I knew the answer."

"Me, too." She stared at the familiar building, its many windows bright. "There's no return address, no fingerprints, nothing to tell us who the person may be."

"If Grayson couldn't find out, then it's a true dead end. We may never know." Brian shrugged one impressive shoulder. "Only time will tell."

"At least we know we're safe. The past is laid to rest."

"That's a relief for all of us. We can go on from here." Brian opened the door and stepped into the cool night. The air breezed over her, and Belle shivered.

Was it her imagination or did he seem even more distant? His walls had gone up, he looked hewn of granite when he appeared at her side. She'd already opened her car door, saving him from the awkwardness of helping her. She rose to her feet, clutching the door to steady herself. She suddenly felt exhausted, as if she'd run a hundred miles nonstop. Brian didn't speak as he unfolded her walker from the backseat and set it in front of her.

"Tomorrow, then." He stood stiffly. His voice held a tense note. "Guess I'll see you at church."

"Guess so." Poor Brian, trying so hard. She didn't know how to handle this situation between them, either. They were divorced, they were no longer friends, in fact she knew little about his life since they'd parted. There was no future for them. All she could do was try to make this easier for him. "You don't need to see me to the door."

"Are you sure? It's the gentlemanly thing to do."

"You've been more than gentleman enough." She pushed her walker forward, keeping her back straight and proud so he'd never know what this cost her. "The milk shake was great. A real treat. Thanks for being so thoughtful."

"It was nothing." Maybe he blushed a little, she couldn't tell in the darkness.

"Are you kidding? You took me for a treat because you knew I would like it. You could have joined me in my room and told me the news. You didn't have to take me out." Her voice shook a little, betraying her as she navigated the sidewalk. "Will you be staying in Grasslands much longer?"

"Just through the weekend. I leave Monday

morning. At least, that's the plan." He lingered behind her—far behind her, as far as he could politely get.

His actions spoke louder than words. In fact, they shouted at her in a language she couldn't ignore. Brian didn't have feelings for her, he wasn't trying to get close to her or starting to like her all over again. No, he was simply being Brian. Polite, helpful, courteous. It's what he did. It's the man he was. It was the reason she'd fallen so hard for him as a teenager, her first love.

"I'm sure the kids will be sorry to see you go." She was just making small talk now, feeling the distance grow between them with her every step. "I know they want you in their lives."

"Thanks, Belle." He stayed back, a man alone in the shadows. "I'll see you tomorrow."

"Tomorrow," she agreed. She said nothing more, not even good-night, as she walked away from him. The automatic doors wheezed open and she stepped through them.

She didn't look back.

The sight of Belle walking away stuck with him on the drive to the ranch and troubled him all through the night. The image snuck into his dreams and it crept into his mind when he opened his eyes come morning. Hours later as the midmorning light shone across the rugged beauty of the Texas landscape, he leaned his forehead against the kitchen window and tried to blot the image of her from his mind. It didn't work.

"Dad, are you okay?" Grayson called out—but when Brian turned around, he saw right away it wasn't Grayson, but Jack.

Warmth spread through him. Getting to know his lost son was icing on the cake. He shoved away from the window. "Just admiring the view."

"It's quite a view," Jack agreed. He looked dashing in his suit and tie. "We're leaving for church. Want to ride with us?"

"Count me in." He couldn't miss the chance to spend time with his boy. "I'm ready. Just need to grab my coat."

"Grayson and Carter are coming along, too." Jack led the way through the house. Brian couldn't seem to forget he'd be seeing Belle in church. The thought brought up feelings he was fighting to keep buried, feelings that *had* to stay buried.

The ride to town was jovial. Comfortable in Jack's roomy double-cab truck, he listened to the brothers converse, banter and jest. It was particularly gratifying to watch them rib each other about their respective lady loves. Having the boys together again meant every jagged piece of his life had clicked into place. He felt deeply moved by the sight of the local church with its white steeple and the crowd of worshippers flocking to the front door. He had so much to be thankful for.

And Belle, his heart seemed to remind him. There she was, settling into a pew with the girls. Every movement she made was graceful, unhampered by her injury. She stood willowy and lovely in a dark, expensive pantsuit, her auburn hair catching the light like sunlit bronze.

His feet cemented to the aisle. He couldn't take a step closer. He fought the need to escape, to dash out the door and drag in some crisp, fresh air.

"Dad, are you all right?" Grayson asked, concerned.

"Fine, sure." What he needed was a few minutes to get his feelings under control, but he didn't have the luxury. The boys surged around him, eager to greet their mother. The rise of their greetings, their hello kisses and hugs lilted through the air like music.

"This will be our first time in church as a whole family," Violet said, reaching out to take his hand.

Affection for his daughter brimmed over and unglued his feet from the floor. He was helpless against the pull of fatherly love and he joined her on the pew, realizing too late that Belle was on his other side.

"Look, it's Sadie." Maddie, on the far end, hopped up and disappeared into the crowded aisle.

"Sadie," Violet informed him, "is our church secretary. We love her."

"You girls are meddling," Grayson told her gently.

"How are they meddling?" Belle wanted to know, but no one answered because a lovely young woman with long blond hair and hazel eyes waltzed up to them.

"Keira." Jack hopped to his feet, turning toward the tall, slender woman. The affection alighting his face said it all. This was the woman who'd captured his heart. He held out a hand, and when their fingers touched anyone could see the love between them was true. "Good to see you, darlin'. Come meet my dad. Dad, this is Keira Wolfe."

"It's great to finally meet you." Keira turned her beaming smile to him. She looked like a sweet thing, just right for Jack. "It must be so good to be home. I know how worried everyone has been. It's a blessing to have you here safe and sound."

"It's good to be here, and to meet you." He scooted down with everyone else to make room for the newcomer, as Keira exchanged pleasantries with Belle. Anyone could see the two had great regard for each other.

"Hey, Elise." Grayson stood up, extending his hand to the striking woman approaching the pew. She had honest eyes and dark, wavy hair. "You look so beautiful."

"And you are handsome, all dressed up for church." She gazed at Grayson with adoration, and it was what any father wanted to see. A grade-school-aged boy stayed by her side. Undoubtedly her son, Cory, who Grayson had mentioned.

"Mr. Wallace." Elise cast her gaze on him. "I'm so excited to meet you. Cory and I couldn't wait to come to Grasslands to see the man that Grayson has told us so much about. I hope you could feel our prayers when you were missing. Everyone was so concerned. That tells me how much you are loved."

"I've heard great things about you, Elise. Grayson is a blessed man to have you." He liked that she blushed. Anyone could see she was a perfect match for Grayson. The family greeted her and Cory warmly, including Belle. Belle clearly felt close to Elise, too. "Hi, Cory."

"Hi, sir," the little boy replied, as cute as could be.

"Look who I found." Maddie returned with a

mousy blonde woman in tow. "I begged Sadie to come over and say hi, and see for herself how Mom is doing."

"I'm well, as you can see," Belle spoke up. "Sadie, nice to see you again. You are adored at Ranchland Manor."

"You two know each other?" Violet asked.

"We met at the convalescent center." Gentle Sadie gave her big glasses a push up her nose. "I do like reading to the people who have no family there. Belle, I'm so thankful you are well enough to come to church. I've been praying for you so hard."

"I've been praying for you, my dear." Turning to Brian to explain, Belle dazzled him with a smile. "Sadie is fairly new to our town. We have enough room for her to join us, right, guys?"

"Sure," everyone called out, scooting down the pew since Elise and Cory needed room to sit, too.

"Oh, I couldn't. Not on your first day back to church." Sadie bit her bottom lip, glancing at him nervously. Poor girl, seemed unusually timid.

"That's Brian Wallace, our father," Maddie pointed out. "Sadie, sit with us. Mom, do you think we should invite her to Sunday dinner?"

"Yes," Violet called out.

"Good idea," Grayson chimed in.

"Please hang with us," Belle invited.

"No, I couldn't impose." Sadie stumbled backward. "But your offer means more than you know."

"Then maybe another time?" Maddie asked, disappointed.

"Definitely." Sadie skittered off, as shy as a church mouse. It was easy to see his family cared for her.

"I hate that she's so alone," Maddie said.

Violet nodded pensively. "She's such a nice person...."

"And so are you." Landon Derringer broke out of the crowd milling in the aisle. It was a bit disconcerting to see him with Violet, when the man had always vowed to marry Maddie. But as he settled down at Violet's side, Brian could see the two went together in a way that Maddie and Landon never had. Another perfect match.

"Sadie is a total sweetheart. Next time I see her at the convalescent center, I'll do my best to talk her into coming to dinner," Belle decided with the jut of her chin that meant she wouldn't take no for an answer.

"We'll leave it to Mom." Violet laughed knowingly.

"Yeah, poor Sadie doesn't have a chance," Maddie agreed, smiling lovingly at her mother.

Brian's gaze flicked to Belle. A pleased little smile clung to the corners of her lush mouth, but he wasn't fooled. She cared deeply about oth-

ers, and he could tell there was something about
Sadie that worried her. Belle's generous heart
was as big as Texas. It touched him now, seeing the kind of woman a man could spend his
life with.

And you blew it, he reminded himself as the
family turned to greet another new arrival. The
church had filled up, ringing loudly with conversations, making it hard to think. As Maddie
dashed down the aisle, excited to greet someone
she spotted in the crowd, he tried to rein in his
feelings for Belle, feelings he didn't dare look at.

Maybe because he didn't need to. He already
knew what they were. So much for keeping the
past in the past. He'd crossed a line. He was no
longer thinking of Belle as off-limits.

Voices around him startled him, cutting into
his thoughts. Everyone stood up to greet Ty Garland and his daughter, Darcy. Ty, the ranch foreman, was received like family and shook Brian's
hand. Easy to see he was a good man, and the
way he gazed at Maddie with absolute love won
Brian over instantly. Belle clearly approved the
match, whispering something soft and light in
the man's ear when he knelt to ask her how she
was doing. She also made a point of raving over
his little girl's new purple dress.

Belle. She stayed front and center in his mind.
He could not look away as the organ music

began, lilting over the resounding conversations. Folks began taking their seats, conversations slowly quieted and he tried to shore up his defenses. Remember the failed marriage. She was his ex-wife who'd divorced him. The twins' mother. But that didn't do it. All he could see was beautiful Belle.

Why couldn't he marshal his defenses? And what had happened to the barriers around his heart? Where was his cool, distant objectivity when he needed it?

"Dad." Carter slid in on the other side of the bench, leaning over Violet and Landon. "I want you to meet Savannah."

"Hello, Mr. Wallace." The beautiful woman with honey-brown hair and green eyes greeted him warmly, clearly in her third trimester of pregnancy. He recalled the sadness in Carter's eyes when he told him of how her estranged husband had died in battle. But judging by the way Carter gazed at her with devotion, he seemed to have made peace with the past.

"It's great to meet you, Savannah. Call me Brian." Pride in his family lifted him up as Reverend Jeb Miller cleared his throat and the congregation silenced.

"Look at our kids. We did good, didn't we?" Belle leaned in to whisper.

"Somehow," he admitted, stumbling over the word because Belle took his breath away.

He didn't know if he could ever get it back.

Chapter Seven

"And this is the barn." Jack led the way into the modern structure, full of roomy box stalls and curious horses watching him over their gates. Behind them he caught sight of well-manicured paddocks where the animals could run and graze, and beyond that a hundred head or so of cattle lounging in the midday sun.

"Impressive." Brian kept pace with his son, following him down the main aisle where horses nickered and a few tried to grab hold of his jacket. "You have quite an organization here."

"We try." A note of satisfaction knelled in Jack's voice. He stroked a horse's nose; his easy way with the animal told Brian something new about his son.

"You have your mother's touch with animals." There he went, thinking of Belle again. It seemed inevitable, so why spend any more energy fighting it?

"That's what I hear." Jack shrugged off the compliment. Things were uneasy between them. They were still almost strangers, after all. "Mom is the one who took over this place when she inherited it from Uncle James. She made it into the world-class operation that it is. Our cattle are some of the finest around. That was her doing. I just took over the reins."

"I don't believe that for a minute." He wasn't used to being like this, defenses down. Being distant was easier. Maybe that had been the big problem in his and Belle's marriage. He could see that now. He plunged his hands into his jacket and kept walking.

Where to start? There were things he needed to say to his son, but they didn't come easily. What if the opportunity for them to be close was lost? Jack kept strolling away, keeping yardage between them.

"Jack?" A teenager popped into view with eager brown eyes and a mop of brown hair. The boy was a little gangly and tall, as if he'd had a growth spurt recently, and his face still held the last traces of childhood.

I remember when Grayson was that age, Brian thought. When it came down to it, he remembered when he was that young and had lost his heart to Belle.

"Hey, Emmett." Jack offered an easy smile to the kid. "Good to see you here on time. Ready to do a thorough muck on the horse stalls?"

"Guess what? I've already begun." The boy squared his shoulders, as if determined to please. "I pitched out all the straw and shavings. I've scrubbed and hosed down two stalls already. I heard you talking and just wanted to make sure you didn't need anything else."

"Looks like you've got a good start on your work." Jack winked his approval. "We'll make a cowboy out of you yet, kid."

"Awesome." Emmett's earnest smile could win awards. "Well, guess I'd better get back to work."

"Say hi to my dad, first."

"Howdy." Emmett gave his Stetson a tug and disappeared down a side aisle, his boots ringing as he went.

"Looks like you have a good hired hand in that one." Brian saw something else in his son. The ability to manage people and bring out their strengths.

"I do. He's a cowboy in training. I'd better watch out or he'll have my job one day." Jack winked, obviously aware that his voice carried along the rafters and the teenager could over-hear him. His pocket chimed. Jack hauled out his cell and squinted at the text on the screen. "Looks like we've got five minutes to get in the house and washed up. Sunday dinner is almost on the table."

"Good. This fresh air has worked up an appetite." Not to mention the morning in church trying to ignore Belle's presence a hairbreadth away from him. He'd noticed her every breath, her every movement and the sweet notes of her voice as she held the hymnal.

"So, has your mom ever dated anyone?" Why that question popped out when so many others were more appropriate remained a complete and utter mystery.

"Uh—" Apparently startled, that's all Jack said.

"I was just wondering, you know. She raised you alone. There wasn't a male role model in your life?"

"There was James Crawford. But he and Mom never dated. He hired Mom on long ago to work as his housekeeper here. A great guy. He became an honorary uncle to us." Raw emotion filled his voice. "James left the ranch to Mom when he passed away. He was family, and he taught me everything he knew about ranching."

"I'm glad he was there for you, Jack." This type of openness made Brian uncomfortable, but he'd made a vow when he feared he might be dying. God had seen fit to give him this second chance, a chance he couldn't let slip by now. He gathered his gumption and said what was in his heart. "You were a fine little boy, and I'm proud of the man you've turned into. I love you, son."

"Thanks, Dad." Jack worked his jaw, a little surprised. He met Brian's gaze standing straight, and honesty carved his face. "I want to love you, too. I just don't know you that well, but I want to."

"That's what I want, too." It was hard being this open, but he didn't back away.

"I wish you would consider staying here with us for a week or longer. Maybe until Christmas." Jack lifted his chin the same way Belle did when her mind was made up. "We've got room. With you being a doctor, you can advise us on Mom's recovery, and this way you'd be close to us. I'm not the only one who wants to get to know you better."

"Violet." He had a soft spot for his daughter. He supposed every father did. The thought of being part of his kids' lives had him nodding before he had a chance to think it through. He'd be near Belle, too, a shoulder for her to lean on when she came home, but didn't that raise a serious question? "What will your mother think of it?"

"Don't worry, I'll handle it." Jack grinned,

pleased, as he led the way through the gate to the back lawn. "If Mom gets mad, I'll take full blame."

"Not sure I want to let you do that, son." It felt good to be walking side by side with Jack, closer than ever.

"What aren't you sure about?" Another voice called out from the porch, a dulcet alto that speared straight to the chambers of his heart. Belle.

"Mom, what are you doing outside?" Jack deftly changed the subject, shared a wink with Brian and clomped up the steps to his mother's side. "Do they know you are out here?"

"Who would 'they' be?" Belle sat on a patio chair bundled up in her coat, her cheeks pink from the crisp air. "I don't need to be watched like a child."

"Well, someone has to keep an eye on you or you do too much." Jack kissed Belle's cheek. "Look at you, doing too much."

"What am I doing? I'm sitting still. Honestly." Belle rolled her eyes. "I'm perfectly fine. I just wanted to breathe in some fresh air and get a good long look at this place. I miss it like a part of me."

"That's because it *is* a part of you." Jack slid a glance sideways at Brian. "See what I mean?

She's pushing so hard, what if her recovery takes a step back instead of a step forward?"

"I see your dilemma," Brian agreed. "Don't think I can help you. I had no sway when I was married to the woman. What influence do I have now?"

"Excellent point." Belle glanced in his direction, but her eyes didn't meet his. "I'm a handful, I know, but I'm determined to be back here to stay, and soon. This is where I belong."

"It's where we want you." Jack opened the back door. "We miss you like crazy around here."

"Sure you do." Belle's love for the boy wreathed her lovely face. She was incredibly breathtaking. "He has free rein while I'm gone. You can't tell me he doesn't like it."

"No comment," Jack quipped as he disappeared into the house, leaving the two of them alone.

Alone. Brian gulped, wishing the few feet separating him from Belle didn't feel as big as Texas. "You really don't like having me here, do you?"

"It's not that I don't like it." Was that a glint of remorse in her gaze?

A matching one coiled behind his sternum. He slid into the chair next to her. "It's complicated between us."

"No kidding." She stared out at the corral, where horses ran with the wind, manes rippling.

"We need to figure out how to negotiate things with the kids." He hated thinking about it, but their lives would always be separate. "You might want all of them with you on Christmas."

"You know I do." Belle turned to him thoughtfully. "I can't imagine this big house empty come Christmas and no one to celebrate with."

"See? They should be with you." Softer feelings filled him. "I know how much you love Christmas. The decorating and the shopping and the hidden gifts waiting to be put beneath the tree."

"That's decent of you, Brian." Sadness lingered behind her words, sadness she probably thought she was hiding from him.

Not a chance. He could see everything. "I failed you—"

"No, you didn't." Her chin jutted stubbornly again. "At least the failure was half mine."

"But I always wanted you to be happy and I couldn't do it. It's what I still want for you. I want what's best for our children, and they would be happy spending Christmas here. So that's the way it will be."

"What about you?" She hated to think of him alone on that sacred day. "The kids are your family, too."

"Don't you worry about me." Emotion rang in the low notes, full of reassurance, and he flushed. Could she sense his anguish? Could she guess why he was doing this?

"You should have Thanksgiving, then." She shifted on the chair, leaning in, closing some of the distance between them. "Fort Worth is close enough that everyone can troop over your way for Turkey Day."

"I'd like that." He bowed his head, so she couldn't read his face. "Then what about you?"

"I've had Jack and Violet for every Thanksgiving for twenty-five years. If you can give up Christmas, then I can give them to you for Thanksgiving." Belle's goodness shone through, and in spite of his shortcomings, she still had the grace to offer him kindness.

His throat closed up, making it hard to thank her. Fortunately, he didn't have to say more. The door swung open and Violet waltzed onto the porch.

"Food is on the table. C'mon, Mom." She swept past him with a smile and tugged her mother's walker closer. "Let's get you inside. Maddie and I made your favorite lunch."

"Being home with you all is blessing enough, but I won't say no to lasagna." Belle popped out of her chair with surprising agility. She truly was progressing along well with her recovery. He may not be needed around here, after all.

"Come, Dad." A mix of emotions passed over Violet's pretty face. "I set the table, so I made sure you would be sitting next to me."

"I can't think of anything better." He tried to hold his feelings still as Belle swept by him. His every sense trained on her with pinpoint accuracy. He breathed in her honeysuckle scent. The light pad of her gait whispered through him, and her loveliness lit up the day. She ambled away from him, unaware of how he felt.

And that's the way it had to stay.

The happiness from the midday meal lingered as Belle pored through a stack of hardback books in the living room, debating which new releases to take with her back to Ranchland Manor. Noises rang from the kitchen, punctuating the girls' merry conversation as they did the dishes. Sundays were her favorite days, with the peace she felt after church and the togetherness of the family meal. Today had been no exception. The size of the Colby-Wallace family had more than doubled since she'd been in a coma. To see her children happily paired off, following the adventure of love wherever it would take them, made her satisfied in a way she'd never been.

Let their adventures be perfect, she prayed

to the Lord. *Let their love be happily ever after, each and every one.* She did not want them to know the unhappiness of a broken marriage or the utter heartbreak when love died.

Footsteps padded behind her. She didn't need to turn around to know Brian had walked into the family room.

"What are you up to?" The smoky rumble of his voice felt as cozy as the fire crackling in the hearth.

"Choosing something new to read for my days at Ranchland Manor." She slid a book off the shelf and stared at the back cover but her eyes didn't focus enough to read it. "Violet and I share books. She's read so many during the long months I was snoozing."

"Only you could call a coma 'snoozing.'" He strolled closer. "I don't know if it's optimism or what it's called."

"The ability to minimize," she quipped. "It doesn't sound as serious if I was snoozing. Snoozing sounds like something you can recover from lickety-split."

"That's the secret. Positive thinking?"

"Right. Positive and preemptive. I don't let the seriousness of it have any edge. Head injury? I'm over it. What I need to do is get my leg to cooperate so I can go riding again. I saw Mouse in the paddock and it's killing me."

"I'm surprised you didn't launch off the porch and try to saddle her up." Amusement twitched at the curve of his mouth.

"Jack forbade it." She blindly pulled two more books from the shelf and set them on the coffee table with the others. "He said he wouldn't let the girls bring me back for another visit if I disobeyed him in this. My own son, working against me."

"Terrible. You did something wrong with that boy."

"Don't I know it." Her laughter joined his, melody and harmony. Just like old times. "Dinner went well. You and Violet had a chance to talk."

"Only a little. It was hard with everyone talking at once. It was chaos." He looked as if he'd liked it.

"There is always a bit of chaos when two sets of twins are involved." Belle eased onto the couch, facing the fireplace. The flames crackled merrily, giving off soothing heat. "You would have thought things would change after they'd grown up, but no."

"So I see." He took the armchair nearest to her. "Talking, contradicting, laughing, teasing. It's almost as if they were never apart. Violet and Maddie are already best friends."

"It was nice to have everyone over. Once they

start marrying off, this will change. We'll be grandparents."

"Tell me about it. Where did the time go? Yesterday they were babies. Today they are grown with lives of their own." Brian swiped a hand across his face. "*Granddad.* That's going to take some getting used to."

"You can't fool me. You're looking forward to it." Sweet yearning filled her, unexpected and unbidden. Where was that coming from? Her feelings for Brian were strengthening against her will. "You'll make a fine granddad."

"Are you ready to be a meemaw?" Twinkles jumped in his dark, rich irises.

"Oh, you think you're funny, but I am completely ready. The more the merrier. The thought of grandchildren running around here, filling this house with laughter and joy again, that's just what I've been praying for."

"Jack tells me you've been alone all this time. That there was never anyone else."

"Oh, don't read too much into that. We were in witness protection. I never knew when we might get uprooted and moved in the dead of night. I didn't want to make any ties I would have to break." The last thing she wanted was for him to know the truth. She'd never been ready to love again. She didn't want to fail at another marriage. "You didn't have that problem, though. Not long after I woke up from my long snooze, Maddie told me how you'd remarried."

"You were gone, Belle. Never to be seen again." Sadness crept across his face along with a silent apology.

"Hey, I understand. We were divorced. You moved on." Prickles of hurt needled into her heart, but no need to let him know. She sat straighter, defenses snapping up. "You fell in love. By all accounts it was a good marriage. A happy place for the children. It's what I wanted for them."

"Sharla wasn't a replacement for you, Belle." He seemed lost. It was the saddest look she'd ever seen on him, digging at the corners of his eyes. "The kids were so small. We were alone. I struggled until Sharla came along and I took a chance."

"I'm glad." How could she feel resentment and gratitude at the same time? "The kids' memories of her are good ones. You loved her."

"I did." He pushed out of the chair, turned away from her and paced to the window. He stood for a long while, wide shoulders braced and back straight. He let silence come between them. The faint kitchen activity filled the stillness, drowned out by the crackles and pops from the fire. The back door opened with a whoosh, letting cool air breeze into the house. Belle shivered, although the coldness never reached her.

There was the issue between her and Brian, one that could never be bridged. He'd lived without her just fine. He'd gone on to love someone else. And all this while, she'd stayed alone. No man had ever measured up to him. That was the truth. Maybe she hadn't wanted any man to measure up to him.

"Mom." Jack charged into the living room with a thump of boots and vital male energy. "I've got the truck warmed up and ready to go. We need to get you back to the convalescent center."

"Right." She set her chin, refusing to give in to emotion. She summoned up as much dignity as possible. "Maybe next time I come home, it will be to stay."

"That's my prayer." Jack gallantly offered his arm.

"God willing." She ignored the fact that Brian had moved from the window to help her.

Not going to happen, she thought, laying her hand on her son's forearm, and maneuvered around the coffee table. She wasn't going to let Brian in ever again. She cared for him, and that had to stop. She had every reason she needed to convince her heart. This time it had to listen.

"Have a safe trip back to Fort Worth in the morning." She didn't look at him as she took charge of her walker. "Be sure and keep in touch."

"But, Mom, he's not leaving in the morning." Jack seemed pleased. "He's staying here."

"Is that wise? I'm sure he can't put his life on hold indefinitely. What about your patients, Brian?"

"My colleagues are covering them," he explained easily. "I'm often gone, volunteering for the poor, in this country or in less fortunate ones. Another week or two won't matter."

"Or *two?*" No, that didn't sound good at all. What if he was still here when the doctor okayed her release? "Don't get me wrong, I want you to spend time with your kids, but do you have to do it here?"

"Maybe I'd better find a place in town," Brian suggested quietly. Apparently he understood how much this was costing her.

"No, I don't want you staying in a motel, Dad," Jack argued. The boy could be stubborn.

"Maybe it's best. I feel uncomfortable here." Brian shifted closer, so close she could smell the fabric softener on his clothes. "It's confusing for us, Jack. Your mom and I used to be deeply in love long ago. It's hard because we're not."

"I get that." Jack's chin eased down a notch. "Do what feels comfortable for you, but we'd all like you to stay."

"That's hard for a father to say no to. What do you think, Belle?"

"I think it occurs to me that I forgot my books. Would you get them for me, please?" His nearness quaked through her like an aftershock. But why? She certainly wasn't in love with him.

Maybe these were old feelings coming to the surface, the impossible wish of an eighteen-year-old for a second chance. That's all. It wasn't any more serious than that.

"Oh, fine. Go ahead and stay," she invited. The worry lifted like a twenty-pound weight. She offered Brian a genuine smile as he handed the books to Jack. "I've changed my mind, although I'm tempted to charge rent."

"Then send me a bill." He laughed as she knew he would, and when his velvet chuckle rippled through the air, smooth and smoky, she didn't need to worry about the familiar sound. Of course it drew up feelings and remembrances, but from the past. The man did not affect her in the here and now. That's what mattered.

"Don't think I won't. No one gets a free ride around here," she quipped, traveling through the house. She felt light. Relieved. Free. "Girls, I'm leaving."

"Already?" Violet dived around the corner first. "We thought we got to keep you longer."

"There's a three o'clock check-in," Brian explained. "Besides, your mother needs her rest. She has a big day at physical therapy tomorrow."

"Yes, I'm hoping to finally dump this walker." Belle forced a smile, because leaving her family wasn't easy. "I want to trade it in for something easier to travel with."

"But we didn't get to watch the movie we picked out." Maddie charged into the room, drying her hands on a dish towel. "We haven't had enough time with you, Mom."

"I know just how you feel." She hugged her daughters. It felt wonderful to hold them together at the same time, her precious girls. "We'll just watch that movie next time I'm here. Keep praying the doctor will spring me soon."

"I haven't stopped in my prayers for you." Grayson ambled in from playing Monopoly on the table. Elise was there with her son, and Keira gave her a hug while Savannah, Ty and Landon offered her kind goodbyes.

So much love hovered in the room, it made it nearly impossible to step toward the door. She wanted to stay here more than anything. Tears burned in her throat as she spilled out onto the front porch.

"Up you go, Mom." Jack opened his passenger door for her and helped boost her onto the seat. "Here are your books."

"Thanks." She clutched them, giving her something to hold on to. The scent of winter grass, the distant moo of a cow and the endless sweeping landscape called to her like a song. But it was the half circle of people clustering together, waving goodbye, that stole her heart. They were her everything. All that mattered to her.

It's just for a short while, she told herself. It wasn't as if they wouldn't call and text and email and visit. The window was down and she clutched the metal lip of the windowsill, savoring this one last moment as Violet and Maddie huddled together, exchanging private words, and Grayson stood so tall and strong next to boyishly handsome Carter.

"Hang in there." Brian approached the window and covered her hand with his. "It will be just a few more days, a week tops, and you can come back to them for good."

Words failed her as she studied his rugged yet gentle face filled with infinite kindness, and against her will, her soul gave a little sigh.

Chapter Eight

The fact that her soul gave a little sigh was nothing to worry about, Belle decided hours later as she ambled down the hall. The chatter of conversations from the dining room seemed to follow her, accentuating her loneliness and reminding her of the home she'd left behind.

"Belle." A familiar voice startled her out of her thoughts. Sadie Johnson turned the corner, looking windblown and dotted with rain. "A storm is brewing out there. I'm glad you got back before it hit."

"Me, too. But what about you, coming out in it to volunteer? Wouldn't you rather be snug at home?"

"Oh, it's nothing. I get lonely, is all." Sadie dipped her head shyly, but there was something wounded about the young woman that brought out the mothering in Belle.

Maybe because Sadie didn't look to be much older than Jack and Grayson. "You can hang out with me anytime you feel lonely, dear. I've got a stack of new books you might enjoy. I pilfered Violet's bookshelf. She has some excellent titles. Come see if you'd like to borrow one."

"Oh, I couldn't." But the wish for company gleamed in Sadie's sad eyes.

The girl was all alone. She'd moved to town around six months ago, and something about her seemed broken. As if she had no confidence. Belle understood all the ways life could wound a person. Maybe Sadie just needed someone to care about her. "I'd be disappointed if we didn't get to talk. You seem to know my children."

"I've been fortunate to get to know them a lit-tle. They've been very kind to me." Sadie slowed her pace, falling in stride beside Belle. "It's hard moving to a new place. I didn't expect them to be so welcoming to me—" She bit her bottom lip, as if she'd said something wrong. "You know, because I'm a stranger."

"You are part of our church family, so you are no stranger to us," Belle reassured her firmly. "Just someone we like that we don't know well yet."

"That's n-nice of you." Sadie seemed ner-vous. Sweet thing, with her too-large clothes that looked secondhand. A church secretary didn't make much, and here she was scraping by on her own. Belle remembered what that was like.

"With the holiday coming up, do you have any family planning to visit?" She led the way into her room. "Or are you traveling to see them?"

"No, I have no family." Sadie shrugged as if it was not a big concern. "My mother died when I was very small, and my f-father, well, he wasn't in the picture."

"I'm sorry to hear that. My parents rejected me when I found myself pregnant at sixteen." Belle tried to imagine Sadie's life. "I understand how it feels to be alone. Who raised you?"

"I was in foster care." Sadie stood off to one side. Maybe being a foster child explained her behavior, always expecting to be on the periphery. "It's taught me there's nothing more important than family, than being together."

"I agree. I'm sorry you weren't able to have that as a little girl." Belle lifted the stack of hardbacks from her nightstand and set them on the foot of the bed for Sadie to peruse. "But you don't have to always be alone. You have your church family. You have friends. Maybe one day you will meet the right man, fall in love and have a family of your own."

"Oh, that would be nice." A whisper of hope turned into a wistful smile. "But probably it's not meant for me."

"You just never know. You deserve to be loved, too, Sadie."

Instead of agreeing, the young woman dipped her chin, and her mousy hair tumbled down to hide her sweet face. She'd grown up without a mother's love—maybe without love of any kind.

Maybe You could watch over her, Father. She sent up a silent prayer. *Help Sadie find the love she deserves.*

"You have some good reading ahead of you." Sadie changed the subject brightly. "This is my favorite author. I recommend you start with her book. I'm sure it's great."

"You haven't read it yet?" Belle took the volume thoughtfully. "Then you should borrow it."

"No, I couldn't. I just c-couldn't." Sadie seemed jittery. She glanced at the doorway. "Maybe I'd better go."

"Please take it." She suspected Sadie might not have a lot of room in her budget for the newest releases of hardback books. "I heard Mrs. Kettle down the hall is a big fan of this author, and she loves it when you come to read to her."

"I was going to see her this evening." Sadie chewed her bottom lip. "She would enjoy the book, I think."

"I think so, too. Go ahead and take it." Belle handed over the volume. "For Mrs. Kettle's sake."

"Oh, this will make her happy." Sadie was

impossible not to adore. "Thanks, Belle. I'll get this back to you as soon as I can."

"No rush. Take your time reading to Mrs. Kettle. Savor every word."

"Oh, I will. Have a lovely evening." Sadie headed toward the door, scurried into the hall and out of sight.

Alone, Belle collapsed onto the side of her bed. The springs squeaked and she sat there, her thoughts boomeranging back to Brian. In the quiet of her room, she missed all her family. And yes, she missed him.

"Dad, I brought you an extra blanket." Maddie knocked on the door and slipped into the den. "It feels like it's going to be cold tonight."

"It's storming hard outside. I'm glad Grayson, Elise and Cory decided to stay here for the night instead of driving back to Fort Worth in this weather." Sleet pounded against the window and wind whapped against the siding as Brian faced his daughter. He had so much to say to her, as he always did, but when it came down to it, words escaped him. "I appreciate the invitation to stay. I know it didn't come just from Jack, but from all of you."

"How could we not want you to stay? We missed you. You were gone for so long."

"Not longer than usual. Remember those ten months I volunteered in the Sudan?"

"Yes, but this felt longer somehow. Maybe it was all the worrying." A weak smile passed over her face. She looked hesitant. Perhaps she had much to say to him, too. This pattern between them, between him and his children, was something he had to break before it was too late.

"I didn't mean to worry anyone." He took the blanket from her, the quality wool soft against his fingertips. He set it on the arm of the sofa.

"I know you were ill and couldn't contact us, but I wish I could have been there for you." She folded her hands together, studying her fingers instead of meeting his gaze.

The old Brian would have taken the chance to back away from talking about feelings. Not this time. "I'd have liked that, too, honey. I did a lot of thinking while I was sick. I missed you a lot."

"You did?"

"Of course." The surprise that filled her eyes pained him. "You're my little girl. I'm always going to love you to the moon and back."

"That's what you used to say when I was young." She moved in to grab the fireplace poker. "When you put me to bed, remember? You'd kiss my cheek and turn out the lights."

"It's something Belle used to say to you."

"Not Mom—I mean, Sharla?" Until she'd

learned about Belle, Sharla had been the only mother Maddie remembered.

"It's too bad you don't remember Belle's love. The way she rocked you through the night when you were sick or teething or colicky. The absolute rapture on her face when she held you for the first time."

"She's so easy to fall in love with. I'll always love Sharla for being a good mother to me, but it's nice to have a mom again." Maddie swiped at tears pooling in her eyes. "Do you mind?"

"That you love Belle? It's what I've always wanted for you. I never thought it was possible." He fisted his hands, determined to say what was on his mind. "God has given us a second chance in more ways than one. He's brought us all together, and He helped me through my illness so I can try and be a better man. I know I wasn't the best father."

"Daddy, you're a fine father." Maddie blinked, her eyelashes damp from unshed tears. "Where did you get the idea you weren't?"

"It's no secret I'm not the warmest person. Your grandmother raised me to have a stiff upper lip, keep emotions in, never show my soft side, and I'm sorry I clung to that way of coping, especially after losing Belle, Jack and Violet. A part of me died."

"Oh, Daddy." Suddenly she was in his arms,

his precious child, the baby he'd cherished, the little girl he'd adored and the young woman he was proud of.

"I love you so much," she whispered against his shoulder.

"I love you to the moon and back," he told her, hating how quickly she left his arms, no longer the little girl who used to run up to him with a baby doll or a new drawing to show him.

"Good night, Daddy." She lingered in the threshold for a moment, but this time the silence wasn't filled with words unspoken. The silence resounded with a quiet understanding, a sense of forgiveness and hope for the future.

"Good night, sweet Maddie," he said as she left him alone with the fire crackling and sleet drumming at the windows.

"What do you think?" Jack asked the others seated around him in Carter's bedroom. He kept his voice low so sound wouldn't carry, not that he worried about disturbing Brian downstairs. The ranch house was big and well built, so it was the conversation itself that warranted whispers. A topic that troubled him greatly. Was Brian Wallace really their father?

The biting accusation from Patty Earl that her husband, Joe, had fathered the boys—not

Brian—had troubled the siblings to the point that Jack and Gray underwent a DNA test.

"He's exactly what you said he was," Violet spoke up, smiling at her twin sister beside her on the floor. The two sat side by side, identical down to the last freckle. "Brian is thoughtful and kind and solid. He's more open than I expected."

"For me, too." Maddie brushed a strand of auburn hair out of her eyes. "He's always been so distant."

"It's just his nature," Grayson spoke up. "I understand more now. It wasn't just losing Sharla that shut him down. It was losing you two."

"And Belle," Carter spoke up. "I think he cared about her more than he'll ever admit. She was his first love."

"That's a lot to lose," Maddie agreed thoughtfully. "He's really trying to be closer to us."

"He's a great guy," Violet agreed. "But is he your real father?"

"I can't see Mom lying about that." Jack raked his hand through his hair. "Mom isn't like that. She might refuse to tell the truth, as in revealing who our father was, but she was protecting us. She referred to Brian as our father. I have to believe her."

"But what about the rumors?" Grayson raked his hand through his hair, identical to his twin. "A father isn't necessarily biological. Maybe Joe

Earl really was our biological father, and Brian never knew the truth."

"I can't see Belle tricking Brian the way Patty Earl said she did." Carter added his opinion, shaking his head, looking pretty certain. "I haven't known her long, but she's amazing. I just can't buy the rumor that Belle tricked Dad into thinking he'd gotten her pregnant when he hadn't."

"No, I agree, but maybe Dad knew," Maddie conjectured. "Maybe he loved Belle enough to marry her and claim her twins as his own."

"Dad has a big enough heart for that," Grayson agreed. "It's love that makes someone a father."

"Biology doesn't have to play a part," Jack added. "So where does that leave us?"

"I think Mom is still too fragile to deal with this." Worry for her mother pinched Violet's face. "That leaves only two choices. We either open the DNA test results now, or we wait until Mom is stronger."

"We'd better wait, because if I read the results right now, how am I going to be able to keep it from her? This is life-changing information." Jack blew out a breath, frustrated. What was the right decision? "I agree, Mom is still too fragile. No way will I do anything to set back her recovery."

"I agree," Grayson spoke up. "Are you all good with that?"

Everyone nodded. It looked like finding out if Brian was their biological father would have to wait a little longer.

Sleet and gray skies hung on for four days. Belle counted each day, gazing out the window longingly every time she got the chance. One thing she was not doing was thinking of Brian. She did everything she could to keep him off her mind by staying busy, working extrahard between her physical therapy sessions and spending time helping her new friends with their jigsaw puzzle.

"I see you traded in your walker." Helga looked up from the nurses' station. "Way to go, Belle."

"It's going to be hard to stop me now." Her cane tapped a rhythm as she walked down the corridor. "Did you hear the news?"

"That you're going home today? Indeed." Helga smiled. "This is very good news."

"The best." She wasn't sure her feet actually touched down as she sailed toward the common room. "I'm packed and ready to go. Just waiting for my ride."

"We'll miss you, dearie." Eunice Lundgrin looked up from the nearly finished puzzle on the common room table. "Things will be dull without you here."

"You still have Anna. She's the real life of the party," Belle quipped.

"I am, it's true," replied the very proper Anna, squinting at a puzzle piece. "Maybe we ought to feel sorry for Belle."

"That's right. She's leaving and we'll still be having all kinds of fun," Marjorie teased.

"I'm going to miss you all." She spent time saying goodbye, making promises to keep in touch and giving final hugs before heading back to her room. All packed, she sat at the window watching the black sheet of clouds spit out a few raindrops.

"Mom." Maddie breezed through the door. Her daughter, not Brian, had come to escort her home. She hadn't realized how worried she was about that.

Belle let out a breath she didn't know she'd been holding. Before she could answer, Violet waltzed in, too. Identical faces, so beautiful and dear. Belle was blown away seeing them together. It would never get old. She held out her arms.

"Come here, you two." She pulled them into a hug.

"How does it feel to be going home?" Violet asked, stepping back, taking a good long look.

"It feels like an early Christmas gift." There were no words. She'd been packed and ready to go since she'd received word from the doctor first thing.

"You look better this morning. Like my old mom."

"Not so old, I hope. Forty-three isn't exactly ancient," she joked. But she understood what Violet meant. "It's been a long six months."

"For us, too," Maddie agreed. "We didn't know if we'd get you back. I prayed for a chance to know you."

"God is good." She brushed hair out of Maddie's eyes and did the same for Violet. Maybe there was no need to grieve the years she'd missed with Maddie, because she could see that the time ahead was filled with infinite joy. This moment marked a new start for all of them. "Take me home, girls."

"Our pleasure," they said in unison, laughing at their twin moment.

"I know Jack is busy running the ranch," she said, crossing the room where her two small bags sat on the foot of the bed. "And Grayson is at his job in Fort Worth."

"And Carter is driving the getaway car." Violet grabbed one bag.

Maddie grabbed the other. "Dad was going to try to make it, but he's busy at the clinic."

"The clinic? So he went back to Fort Worth after all." Good. That was a relief. He had a life there, it's where he belonged. It really was a great thing she wouldn't be seeing him. She swallowed past her disappointment. Really, it was for the best.

"Oh, no, Dad's volunteering at the clinic here." Maddie took one glance around the room to make sure they had everything.

"The Grasslands Medical Clinic next door?" That made no sense at all. "You mean, *right next door?*"

"That's the one. He's doing more mission work and set up free clinic days this week for the poor." Violet opened the closet and pulled out Belle's overcoat. "Here, put this on. It's freezing out."

"He's been right here in Grasslands this week?" She couldn't exactly say why she wasn't processing that information. Talking with him on Sunday had made everything clear. She shouldn't be feeling so shook up. He hadn't visited, and maybe that was the right move. Good decision on his part. "Right next door?"

"That's what we said, Mom." Violet helped Belle into the coat as if she were the child. "We know you're not exactly happy with him staying at the house."

"It's not that I'm unhappy. It's more like we

already have a full house." She fumbled with the buttons. Having her ex-husband live in the same house with her for a bit, no, that wasn't weird at all. "Exactly how long is he staying?"

"Long enough, we hope." Violet led the way into the hall.

"Take one last look around. This is a big occasion, Mom." Maddie hesitated in the doorway. "You beat the odds, you're walking on your own and you're going home."

"I don't think it was me." She was more overcome than she wanted to admit. "It was the Lord. You kids and your love also got me through."

"We prayed for this day." Violet walked backward slowly, waiting for them to catch up. "Another prayer answered. God has been busy."

"And we're so grateful," Maddie added.

"Yes, we are." She was going home. Belle called out goodbyes as she passed rooms, waving to Marjorie and Anna and Eunice, promising to keep in touch.

The moment she turned the corner, she spotted him. She wasn't looking for him intentionally, but her gaze naturally zoomed to where Brian stood at the front counter, chatting with Doc Garth. His friendly baritone floated to her, drawing her forward. His back was to her, but he turned as if he knew her footsteps above all others, his gaze zeroing past the girls straight to her.

Good thing she jerked her eyes toward the tile floor at the last moment, avoiding the piercing connection. She didn't look up until she'd reached the front counter, where the girls stopped to join Brian and the doctor in conversation.

"Belle, we weren't sure this day would come." Doc Garth scrawled his signature on a clipboard and handed it to the receptionist. "Praise God that it has. You can go home. How does it feel?"

"Freeing." She avoided looking at Brian as she tried to catch her breath. "I've been penned in too long. I'm like a mare yearning to gallop."

"You keep your physical therapy appointments, and you'll be galloping as fast as you ever did in no time at all." Pleased, Doc Garth walked her to the front door. It rasped open to the cold wintry day. "Call if you need anything. Girls, if you have a question, you have my number. Not that you'll need it with Brian around, but know that you're always welcome to chat."

"Thanks, Doc," the twins said in unison, as sweetly as a song.

"I'll make sure she follows your instructions," Brian promised, bringing up the rear of the group. Belle followed with impressive speed, her auburn hair swishing with her brisk gait.

She couldn't be prettier, even in jeans and a black peacoat, the flash of her copper-colored cane marking her progress like a metronome.

Her leather boots padded straight to Violet's SUV, where the girls fussed and got her settled into the front seat while he shivered in the cold, not knowing if he should lend a hand or not. Belle didn't seem to want him to. Her avoidance of him spoke volumes.

He didn't blame her. He was trying to keep a respectful distance between them, too. Long ago he'd disappointed her in the worst way by not being the husband she deserved. How could he forgive himself? Belle had found happiness in her life without him. As much as that hurt, it was what he wanted for her.

"You girls call me once you get her home. And let me know how she's doing." He couldn't help caring, couldn't stop wanting to help. "Not that there should be any problems, but you know her."

"She'll overtire herself without meaning to." Violet nodded as Maddie shut the door, closing Belle inside the car.

"Yes, that's what she'll do." He spotted her through the windshield, and his heart stalled. She was still the most striking woman he'd ever seen—inside and out. She'd always amazed him. She still did. She'd left with nearly nothing the night witness protection had whisked away her, Violet and Jack, and built a life to be proud of. Her prosperous ranch, her beautiful children. He admired her one hundred percent.

"We'll see you for supper?" Violet asked, jingling her keys as she opened her door.

"Yes." He plunged his hands in his coat pockets. The wind gusting against him smelled like rain.

"See you tonight, Dad." Maddie settled into the backseat and he stepped forward to close the door for her.

Inside the vehicle, Violet started the engine, and he caught sight of Belle behind the glass, her lustrous hair framing her oval face. Her dark gaze caught his. She gave a little finger wave as the car pulled away. He waved back, watching them leave. He'd never felt more alone.

Chapter Nine

"Mom, are you awake?" A light rap in the dark startled Belle from her slumber.

Apparently she'd been napping. She was stretched out on her bed, covered with a wool throw while the TV mounted on the facing wall murmured the evening news. "I only meant to close my eyes."

"Well, you've had them closed for nearly three hours." Violet sailed into the room. "Lupita has supper ready."

"I smell her enchiladas. How I've missed them." She pushed up into sitting position, sniffing the air faintly redolent of cheese and spices. "Did she make her Spanish rice?"

"And refried beans. She went all out for your first meal home."

"I need to thank her. That woman is like family."

"She had to leave early. She had a church thing."

Violet rescued the cane from where it leaned against the wall. "Don't tell me you left this over here and walked all the way to the bed without it."

"It was what, three or four steps?"

"You're cheating, Mom. The doctor said not to push too hard, that could backfire on you. You don't want your leg to stay like this, right?" Violet held out the cane.

"Don't think for one second our roles have reversed, young lady." Although she was proud of Violet, who had come into her own. "I'm the one who gives orders around here."

"Sure, sure. We'll see how that works for you." Amusement quirked the corners of her mouth. Violet nearly always smiled these days. Love could do that to a girl.

"Will Brian be eating with us?" She took the cane and stood, obediently using the thing properly, the way her physical therapist had shown her. "Or will he be busy at the clinic?"

"He's only working mornings." Violet shrugged. "That's all I know. So yes, he'll be here to enjoy Lupita's enchiladas, which are not to be missed. Let's get you downstairs."

"I don't need a nanny, sweetheart. Go ahead without me. I'll be down in a minute."

"Okay, you just look tired, Mom. You came

home, you wanted to do this and see that and wound up doing too much walking."

"That's not why I'm tired, honey." She shuffled her lethargic left leg forward, not sure she wanted to talk about some of the things weighing on her. "I have a lot on my mind. Do you forgive me for not telling you about your dad?"

"I understand why, but honestly, all this time I thought he had abandoned us. It would have helped to know that he didn't want to let us go. That somewhere out there he still cared for us."

"Cared? He loves you very much. It's why Maddie and Grayson stayed with him. How could I ask him to give up all his children?" She sighed heavily. "I know he loves you as much as I do. It would have killed me to lose all four of you. I didn't want him to lose that much."

"I do understand. You couldn't risk Jack and me trying to find our dad."

"Or your other halves." Belle hesitated at the top of the stairs, which were tricky. She gripped the banister with her free hand, holding tight. "So you really forgive me?"

"I was never mad at you." Violet stayed close, the love in her eyes obvious. "Is your leg wobbling?"

"It's fine. Getting stronger every day." She tried not to remember all the thousands of times she'd raced up and down this staircase in a hurry to get to one thing or another, always busy. Those times would come again, she was sure of it. She reached the bottom step and gave a sigh of relief.

"Mom, there you are." Jack strode in, smelling of hay and winter wind. He'd obviously just finished feeding, one of her favorite things to do around the ranch. Hauling hay, forking it out, measuring grain and taking time with the livestock. Those times would return for her again, too. "We don't want dinner to get cold. Lupita pulled out all the stops. It's good to have you home."

"It's good to be here." Although the dining room was near, she could hear the drone of conversations through the wall. She took Jack's hand. "Go on, Violet. We'll be right there."

"Okay." Violet exchanged looks with her brother before sauntering away, disappearing through the doorway.

"I wanted to check and see how you're feeling, son." She drank in the sight of him. He'd grown tall and strapping over the years, capable and responsible. A true man. She couldn't be more proud. "You're not still feeling responsible for my fall, right?"

"I never meant for you to get hurt, Mom. If I hadn't pushed so hard—" He stopped, shook his head, scattering chestnut-brown hair. His golden-brown eyes winced with emotion. "Maybe I should have trusted you more when it came to Dad. I should have known there was a good reason you couldn't tell us about him."

"I should have at least let you know that much, that there was a good reason. I was just afraid for our safety." She rubbed a hand up his arm, the way she used to do when he was small. A comforting gesture. "As for the fall, you know I've gone heels over head off Mouse before. How many times have I been tossed from a horse?"

"A few. Remember that stallion you broke?" His face crinkled with a fond smile. "We lost count of how many times you hit the ground."

"See? I could have gotten hurt then, but I didn't. This one time, I landed wrong. Trust me, I know how to fall off a horse." She gave his arm a squeeze. "Not your fault in the slightest. Got it?"

"I do." Swallowing hard, he nodded toward the dining room. "Now let's eat."

All was well, so she followed his suggestion, trudging her way to the doorway where the sight stole her breath. Her family greeted her from around the table and she treasured their smiling faces, their love and laughter, their joy and applause as she ambled in. She beamed happily at Ty and Darcy, as well as Jack's fiancée, Keira, and a very pregnant Savannah, delighted to see that they were all taking part in the family celebration. Her only regret was that Gray's and Violet's sweethearts were back in Fort Worth.

Brian stood up and pulled out her chair. "Now that you're home, the kids have plans for you," he explained as she eased onto the cushion.

"Plans? Ooh, now I'm afraid." She tried not to let his gentlemanly gesture affect her. Getting her chair was something he'd always done when they'd been married. Out of respect for her, he'd said then. He'd really been a sweet young man, but she knew that wasn't the case now. It was likely because of his polite nature, that was all, so she didn't feel too self-conscious as she smiled up at him. "Do I dare ask what kind of plans?"

"Brace yourself." His dark eyes glittered with mischief.

"Did you hear her?" Maddie asked her siblings. "She asked what kind of plans."

"As if she doesn't know," Jack scoffed lightly, taking the chair at the foot of the table.

"Christmas plans. What else?" Violet chimed, shaking her head of auburn hair. "Honestly. This is the Colby household, well, the Colby-Wallace household now, and we know how to do Christmas."

"What Christmas?" Grayson asked, tongue-in-cheek. "I don't see Christmas here."

"Exactly my point," Violet answered, while

Carter shook his head, watching the twins' exchange with good humor.

"We've got to do something about that," Maddie declared. "Fortunately, we have a plan to make this house more Christmassy."

"Yippee!" Darcy exclaimed.

"Starting tomorrow," Violet agreed, smiling at Ty's daughter. "Two o'clock. Gray, you can be there, right?"

"I'm counting on it," he affirmed. "Can't wait."

"This Christmas will be the way all the rest should have been," Maddie spoke up. "We'll be together, at last."

While the twins chattered on, discussing who would say grace, Brian leaned in to whisper, "You sighed."

"I did?" She felt as if her world had suddenly righted. "Do you know how many times I dreamed of this?"

"I did, too." His nearness felt comfortable, his smile the most reassuring thing she knew.

Her affection for him brightened, sweet and adoring. She didn't know how to hold it back.

"Who knew an impossible dream could come true?" he asked.

"God did," she said, and they smiled together. Jack began the blessing and she bowed her head, but the smile and the brightness within remained.

* * *

Who knew an impossible dream could come true? Brian's question stuck with him through the meal and whispered at the back of his mind as the evening passed with first a game of Scrabble and then watching a medical drama with the family. Now, hours later, another question troubled him as sleep eluded him. Could the Lord have another impossible dream in store for them?

I wish, he thought, but he couldn't see it was likely. He'd lost his chance with Belle long ago.

He tossed, even though the firm cushions gave him plenty of support. It was a comfortable couch for sleeping and not the reason he shoved up onto his elbows to squint across the room at the luminous alarm clock Violet had dug up for him. Eleven minutes past midnight. Great. He'd volunteered for another day at the clinic tomorrow because there was so much demand. Apparently Grasslands never had a free clinic offered before, and his packed schedule started at seven-thirty.

He sat up all the way, rubbed a hand over his face, and tiredness buzzed through him. He needed his sleep. Maybe some warmed milk would help. He shoved his feet into slippers and grabbed his terry robe, tying the sash as he eased open the door. Hinges whispered as he headed for the kitchen. Faint light from a crescent moon peeked between clouds and spilled through the windows to guide his way.

A muffled clunk echoed through the house. Was someone else up? Curious, he bounded into the dark kitchen and something slammed into his face. Pain shot across his cheek and occipital bone.

"Brian!" The overhead flashed on, clearly illuminating Belle standing on the other side of the open cabinet. "Are you all right? I didn't see you there."

"Because the light was off." Annoyed and glad to see her, yet trying not to show it, he gave the cabinet door a shove. It thudded shut. "What are you doing down here in the dark?"

"I'm trying not to wake up fully. Not that it's any of your business." She waltzed away from him, gorgeous with her satiny hair rumpled from sleep and her floral robe swishing around her. "What are you doing sneaking around my house?"

"I wasn't sneaking. I came in here to heat some milk." His eye stung, but what pained him more was the way she looked tonight. When they'd been married, how many nights had he seen her like this? With her flannel pajamas and robe, her hair mussed, her face smudged with sleep, rocking a baby or two in her arms? "I wasn't the one sneaking. You were the one who didn't turn on the light."

"Neither did you." She grabbed a bag of peas from the freezer. "Next time you're creeping around in the dark of night, turn on a lamp or something."

"I didn't get the chance." Honestly, the woman could drive him crazy. "You hit me with the cabinet before I could reach the switch."

"A likely excuse." Her chin went up, a sure sign she was trying not to laugh. "I didn't hit you. You walked into the cabinet."

"Which you opened in my face." As long as he argued, he didn't have to think about how he wanted to take her in his arms and kiss her until her stubbornness faded and she melted against his chest. "If I didn't know any better, I'd think you hit me on purpose."

"I did no such thing!" Glints of amusement shone as she shoved the frozen peas at him. "Goodness, I did get you good. You're starting to swell."

"I told you." He grabbed the bag and held it to his eye. "It's dangerous taking a walk in this house. It was always hazardous around you, Belle."

"Remember the time I opened the shower door and didn't know you were there?"

"You cracked my nose, and it bled for nearly

an hour." He looked at her with one eye, since the other was covered by the icy bag of peas. "What about the time you left the groceries on the kitchen floor—?"

"I'd just gotten home and the boys were still babies, who both decided to get sick at the same time—"

"And I didn't look down, tripped over the box of laundry detergent and squished a week's worth of vegetables."

"Not to mention what you did to the bag of potato chips." Her laughter rang like a merry bell. "I had splurged on the name brand, too. I had a coupon."

"When the folks I worked with wanted to know why my wife packed a baggie full of potato chip slivers and crumbs to go with my sandwich, I didn't want to admit what happened."

"Because the problem was with you, Brian. You should have looked down." She backed against the counter, hands to her stomach, laughing.

"Yes, it was all my fault," he agreed, chuckling now when he hadn't been able to then. "I can admit it. Back then, I took things too seriously."

"Things *were* serious and I was just so stressed, especially when the girls came along. *Two* sets of twins. Some days I look back and don't know how I managed."

"You did just fine, Belle." Admiration shone in his eye—since the other one was hiding behind the vegetable bag. "You were running full-out day and night trying to take the best possible care of our children."

"You were the same, juggling school and full-time work. Remember when you also took on the janitor job at the church when we had those extra medical bills and we couldn't make our rent?"

"My first introduction to church. Reverend O'Neill was the minister back then, and he was a savior of sorts. It's because of his kindness I turned to the Lord after you and the kids left. I needed prayer. I needed to pray for you."

"You prayed for me?" Touched, she propped her cane against the nearby cabinet and nudged the bag away from his eye. "Oh, this is swelling terribly. I hit you hard. I'm sorry, Brian."

"I'm sorry, too."

For the cabinet door or the past, she couldn't tell which, but it didn't matter. "It's already bruising. You're going to have a black eye for work tomorrow."

"It will make a funny story how my ex-wife attacked me. Everyone will believe it."

"This is a small town, you can't go spreading stories like that." Half-horrified, although she knew he was joking, she gave him a light slap on the chest. "I don't want you letting people think I take out my aggressions on you."

"Sure, because folks will likely believe it."

"Right, because I'm stubborn?" She bit her lip to keep from laughing. "Maybe I'll spread rumors how you deserved it. People will be more likely to believe that."

"I give up, you win." He laughed again with a low, gravelly rumble. "I don't mind you winning, Belle. You know I was kidding."

"I know. I have you figured out." She pressed the peas gently against his bruising eye. "Let me get you something better. I think there are some gel packs—"

She took a step back, her left leg gave way and she let out a yelp as she fell. Brian's iron arms wrapped around her, catching her before she fell. The bag of frozen peas smashed to the ground, her pulse skidded to a stop and she landed safe against the wide plane of his chest.

"Belle, are you—?"

"Yes," she answered too fast, too breathlessly. "I'm—"

"Dad? Belle?" Footsteps padded into the kitchen. Carter stared at them, mouth agape. "Uh, excuse me. I'll just duck out of here. Sorry."

"Carter!" Belle pushed away from Brian's chest.

"Carter." Brian released her. "Wait."

"This isn't what it looks like." Belle grappled for her cane. "I lost my balance—"

"Hey, no need to deny it." Carter held up both hands, an innocent man. "I saw what I saw."

"We're not—" Brian started.

"No way," Belle agreed.

"I didn't mean to interrupt." Carter grinned ear to ear. "You two go back to what you were doing. I'll just retreat to my room—"

"Don't you dare go, young man." Belle hurried toward him. "This is not what it looks like."

"It looked like you and Dad were hugging." Carter grinned wide and turned to look behind him. Grayson stood there, grinning, too. "Caught in the act, I'd say."

"This is an interesting development." Grayson propped one shoulder against the door frame. "What do you think, Violet?"

"About what? I heard a noise and come down here to find y'all in the kitchen." Violet tightened the belt of her robe. "What's an interesting development?"

"Yeah, I missed it." Maddie joined the crowd, running her fingers through her sleep-tousled hair.

"Your mom and our dad hugging." Carter seemed happy to spread that news.

"Hugging?" The girls gasped simultaneously,

casting gazes full of questions Brian's way. "Is it true?"

"No, not exactly." He'd better nip this in the bud right here. "We both wanted some warm milk. That's not against the law the last time I looked. What are you all doing up, when you should be fast asleep?"

"There was a lot of noise down here," Carter explained innocently.

"Yeah, thought it would be wise to investigate," Grayson agreed.

"We heard voices," Violet started.

"And plus we're here because we're nosy," Maddie finished. "Were they really hugging?"

"Maybe kissing. I don't know," Carter reported. "I didn't have a great view and they were awfully close."

"No, no, no." Belle blushed bright red. "See how rumors get started? This is entirely innocent. I bashed your father with the cabinet door. Not on purpose."

"Well, that's debatable," Brian quipped, slipping by her to shoo the children out of the kitchen. "Go away, all of you. Up to bed. I don't want to see you until morning."

"You don't fool us, Dad." Violet patted his arm lovingly. "Your bark is worse than your bite."

"Totally," Maddie agreed, beaming. "We'll

leave you and Mom to do, er, whatever it was you were doing."

"Nothing," Belle called out from behind him. "We were doing nothing."

"A likely story." Violet winked at him before turning on her heels. "At least it wasn't an intruder."

"Really glad I came down when I did," Grayson cracked as he trailed the gang up the stairs.

Only Carter stayed behind, fighting laughter. He leaned in, keeping his voice low. "Belle is great, Dad. I don't know how you ever let her go."

Brian opened his mouth, but no blithe response came. Not one quip, not one gentle joke, just a garbling, strangled silence as his youngest son stalked out of sight, hurrying to join his older siblings. No doubt there would be a big discussion about this upstairs. Not sure what he ought to do about that.

"They have the wrong impression." He whipped around, saw Belle leaning against the counter with a hand to her mouth and almost laughed, too. "They think we were getting lovey-dovey."

"This really is funny." She dissolved into laughter. "Honestly, they are only giving us a hard time. Look at your eye. It's swelling shut."

"I've lost all depth perception."

"You poor thing. Take this back to the den and

ice that eye thoroughly. You have to be able to drive tomorrow." She gave another giggle. "Don't worry about the kids. They have to know we were telling the truth."

"I'm not so sure." He didn't want to argue about it. He didn't want to discuss his feelings for Belle—past, present or future. What he wanted was a cup of warm milk and a good night's sleep so he could wake up to find this was all a dream. That he really hadn't held her in his arms and remembered the bliss of happier times. Their marriage hadn't all been bad.

"Go lie down. I'll heat us some milk and bring you a glass." Belle turned her back, reached in a cabinet and dug out a small pan.

"I'd better get out of here while I can." He opened the fridge and carried the carton of milk to her. "It's not safe in here."

"Right, you wouldn't want me to get your other eye, then both would be swollen shut." Just for an instant the years melted away, and it was like they were young and together again. Her dark gaze glittered mirth and caring. "I'd hate to be the reason people in need didn't receive medical care tomorrow. Now go."

"Right." He couldn't shake the feeling something between them had changed. He left her to her work, listening to her hum a Christmas tune as he headed through the moonlight. No way could they go back, even if they wanted to.

He'd failed her badly by not being able to open his heart. Shame and guilt wrapped around him, keeping him as if in shadow.

Chapter Ten

Why was she so nervous this morning? Belle couldn't explain the pins and needles in her stomach or why she'd sloshed coffee on the kitchen counter. She grabbed the dishcloth and swiped up the spill.

"You should be resting." Lupita scrambled eggs at the stove. "Not standing around trying to lend a hand."

"I'm bored. I have to do something." Belle rinsed the cloth and began cleaning the counter. "Jack refused to let me go out in the fields with him."

"Rightfully so." The older woman gave the eggs a stir. "You were in a coma for nearly six months. Scared us all to death."

"I'm sorry. I didn't mean to worry anyone."

"What do you think you're up to now?" Lupita turned from the stove.

"Trying to make myself useful." But judging by the look on the housekeeper's face, she was failing badly. She obediently returned the cloth to the sink. "Sorry."

"Do you know what? There are too many cooks in this kitchen. Violet, there you are. Will you do something with your mother? Take her to lie down somewhere, dear. I don't care where, just get her out of my kitchen."

"My pleasure." Violet seemed absolutely cheerful this morning. "Mom, what are you doing up so early?"

"Force of habit. The day starts early on the ranch." She allowed her daughter to take her by the arm. "I don't want to be treated like an invalid."

"You are recovering from a serious injury." Violet steered her into the living room. Sun tumbled through wide windows, giving her a view of the Texas meadows she loved so much. "Sit down, I'll fetch your book from upstairs. Put up your feet and relax."

"I'm fine. And you can stop looking around for signs of your father."

"Whatever do you mean?" Innocent as a lamb, Violet swept a lock of auburn hair behind her shoulder.

"Brian left for work an hour ago." She knew because she'd waited upstairs, cracking her door to listen to the sounds drifting up from below, and didn't come down until he was gone. "He had an early morning at the clinic."

"I think it's cool how he donates so much of his time to the poor. Don't you?"

"Who wouldn't?" She didn't want to admit how much she admired him. Brian may have grown up with his wealthy grandmother, but he'd always been clear about what mattered most in life.

"Well, I think he's great." Violet arched a questioning eyebrow. "Don't you?"

"Sure."

"You and he seemed kinda close last night. Maddie and I talked it over. We wouldn't be crushed if you and Dad got along."

"Hey, we get along. We're civil."

"I meant, *get along.* As in, you know…"

"I most certainly do *not* know." She laughed, remembering last night. She wondered how Brian's eye was doing. "There's nothing to it, as you know very well. You can stop teasing."

"Well, it looked like something to me." As lovely as the morning, Violet turned on her heel. "It wouldn't be the end of the world if you and Dad started liking each other again."

"I like him just fine, and liking is as far as I'm prepared to go."

"Okay, believe what you want." Violet stepped happily away.

Alone, Belle turned to study the frosty morning landscape. A thin layer of white coated grasses and painted everything in a crisp sheen. Her thoughts turned to Brian. Last night, being in his embrace again, even for just one moment, had been bliss. She could still remember the steel of his chest, the comforting band of his arms enfolding her and the security she'd always felt when tucked against him.

Stop thinking about the man, she told herself, to no avail. She kept on anyway.

After a busy day at the Grasslands Medical Clinic, Brian said goodbye to his last free patient for the day, thanked Nurse Hamm for her help and retreated to the small break room in the back.

He'd worked nonstop from seven-thirty, with only a few moments to grab a bite of the lunch Lupita had packed for him, bless her. He'd have starved otherwise. Word had gotten around and the clinic waiting room had been packed with walk-ins.

All in all, it had been a good workweek. He finished the bottle of iced tea in his lunch sack. The coolness slid over his tongue, refreshing him. It felt wonderful to get off his feet. He glanced out the small window into the rear parking lot. He could see a corner of the nursing home where Belle used to be.

Belle. What was he going to do about his feelings for her?

"Brian?" Doc Garth paused in the doorway, a stack of charts tucked in the crook of his arm. "It's nice to see you taking a break. I can't believe the work you put in today."

"There's more need for free medical attention than you realize in any community, even one as homey and nice as Grasslands." Brian took another swig of iced tea. "I hope it wasn't too big of a drain on your resources here. Your Nurse Hamm was running as hard as I was. Maybe harder. It was good of her to help me. I hope she didn't feel taken advantage of."

"She's a great nurse, but she knows how to speak her mind." The doc chuckled fondly. "She would have let you know if she objected."

"Good to know. Thanks for offering me a place to offer a little service."

"This week has opened my eyes. There are a lot of people who can't afford medical care, but deserve it." Garth's face creased with thought. "I recognized only some of the patients. It's my guess people came from the outlying areas and rural communities."

"Mine, too. Word spreads."

"It's been a help having another doctor around."

"You've got a fine practice, Garth. You weren't kidding when you said you could use a hand around here."

"My business is growing so much, it's gotten to where I can't handle it alone. I know you have a practice in Fort Worth, but now that you have family in Grasslands, you might want to think about a move."

"I honestly haven't thought that far."

"Well, when you do, I'd like to offer you a place here. Either full-time, or part-time. And to sweeten the deal, we can offer a free clinic day, say the first Friday in every month, for those in need."

"Wow, I can't say that doesn't interest me." Move to Grasslands? His home was in Fort Worth. It was where he'd raised his children and built his life. But Grayson planned on settling down in Grasslands permanently because Elise wanted a small-town upbringing for her son. Maddie seemed blissfully happy and her move here was a permanent one, too. Even Carter had taken to ranch work like a duck to water.

"I'll think about it," he found himself saying. Could he really relocate here? And what about Belle?

Garth looked pleased. "I can't ask for more than that."

"Excuse me, Dr. Wallace?" Nurse Hamm stood in the hallway. "We had a late walk-in. I told her we'd closed for the day, but she drove forty-five minutes to get here. One look at her, and I thought you'd might want to see her."

That couldn't be good.

Brian nodded. "I can make time."

"Then I'll show her to exam room one and get her information. I can stay a little longer, too." Although it was well after four-thirty and she'd already put in a nine-hour day, the nurse strode down the hall without complaint.

"Give a holler if you need a hand." Garth headed to his office to finish his day's paperwork.

Brian pulled out his cell. Caught up at clinic, he typed out. Will B late, but coming. He debated for a moment, his thumb hesitating over Belle's name in his address book before he pressed it. She was the right choice and would let the others know. He pushed himself to his feet and went to meet his patient.

"A woman in her forties, who's put off going to a doctor because she couldn't afford it," Nurse Hamm explained, meeting him in the hall. "She's been fighting what looks like bronchitis for a few weeks. It's taken a bad turn."

He took the chart, glanced at the nurse's careful notes and frowned. "Good thing you let her in. You're a caring nurse."

"Don't I know it." She winked at him before scurrying off to finish her closing-up routine.

He knocked on the exam room door and opened it. Two little fireballs raced around the room, black hair tousled, their giggling peppering the air.

"Boys, calm down," the slender and pale woman hunched on the exam table wheezed out. "I'm sorry, Doctor. My grandsons refused to nap in the car on the drive here. I take care of them while my daughter works."

"I understand. They're overtired and revved up." He knelt as the double images approached him. "Hey, boys. Whatcha got there?"

"A twain."

"A caboose!"

Both boys held up plastic train pieces.

"Choo-choo."

"Whoo, whoo."

They took off again, chugging around the room making train sounds.

"I have twin sons myself." Brian stood and pulled his stethoscope from his pocket. "They're grown men now, but they were like that once. Double the fun, but double the little-boy energy."

"I love them dearly." The grandmother—

Allie—coughed and wheezed. "But some days they wear me out."

"I'd like to tell you that will pass, but not until they are in their twenties."

"I was afraid of that." Allie had kind dark eyes, and she was far too pale. "I suppose you want to know why I'm here. The boys had bronchitis last month."

"And you caught it, too?"

"Yes, but they got over theirs, as you can see. However, I wasn't so fortunate."

"Let me guess." He'd heard the story more times than he could count today. "You couldn't afford medicine for all of you, so you filled the boys' prescription but not your own."

"Guilty." She winced. "I know it was wrong, but I had to make a choice. It was between that and food for the week."

"I understand." He'd been fortunate to inherit a shocking amount of money from his grandmother, who'd passed away just after the girls were born, so he never had to worry about making those choices—and that was the reason he donated his services to those less fortunate. "You couldn't kick the bronchitis on your own, and now you're worse off."

"Exactly."

"Then let me listen to your lungs, see what we're dealing with." He stepped around the boys as they chugged and choo-chooed, and uncoiled his stethoscope. He feared he knew what he would find even before he examined her.

"Mom, did Dad say when he was coming?" Violet pulled her knit hat from her coat pocket in the crispy chill of the town's tree lot.

"No idea. He didn't say." Belle stopped in front of a white fir tree, trying to stay calm. Why should she be nervous? They were only picking out a Christmas tree. Nothing to be uptight about. "What do you think about this one?"

"I like the spruce better," Maddie called over her shoulder, a few paces away. "It's fuller."

"Taller," Carter agreed.

"This is the tree." Jack's voice boomed farther down the aisle.

The twins headed his way, eager to have a look. Belle would let the kids pick—that was part of the tradition. She hung back as the others hurried along the row of trimmed evergreens, her palm so damp she couldn't properly grip the handle of her cane. Fine, so she was nervous. She couldn't help it. She was going to have to deal with Brian again.

Her cell chimed with a text message. She knew it was from him. She fished out her phone and glanced at the screen, wishing her hand didn't tremble.

On my way, he'd written.

The clinic wasn't far, a few minutes away. She tucked her phone in her pocket, trying to calm her heartbeat. These feelings were supposed to be from the past. Remnants, like faint embers burning out. So, why couldn't she calm down?

Because she couldn't forget being in his arms, that's why.

"How are you doing?" Carter swooped in, pure soldier honor, staying at her side. He shot a worried glance at her. "This isn't too much for you?"

"You are a sweetheart, but no need to coddle me." She really did adore the boy. Noble, decent and a real gentleman. "Why aren't you checking out the tree Jack found?"

"Thought you would make better company."

She wasn't fooled. The fact that Brian's son felt protective of her made her love him. That wasn't hard to do, not at all. Even if he was the reminder that Brian had gone on with his life without her and married another. Given his heart to another. Built a life with another woman. She wanted to hold a grudge over that, but how could she? Truly, she was sorry Sharla Wallace had died in a car accident so many years ago. She would have liked to meet the woman who'd been such a good mother to Maddie and Grayson, the woman who'd given Carter life.

She smiled at the boy. "You are so like your father. Savannah is blessed to have you in her life."

"Thanks...but I'm the lucky one." Carter shrugged a brawny shoulder in a casual gesture, just like Brian. "My fiancée's an amazing lady, and I'm so glad you'll be there for our wedding."

"I wouldn't miss it for the world," Belle said warmly.

"What are you two up to?" The one voice she missed most rumbled behind her. "Have you picked out a tree yet?"

"It's likely. I'd better go check." Carter stepped aside. That grin from last night was back, from when he'd found them in the kitchen together. "I'll just leave you two alone."

Belle watched the young man go, and it gave her an excuse not to look at her husband. *Ex*-husband. *Remember that, Belle,* she told herself, but did it do any good? No. When he fell into stride beside her, her gaze slid sideways. He towered beside her, a shadow in the fading daylight. Her spirit lifted at the sight of him. Of his smile. Of his steady, comfortable presence that seemed to drive the chill from the air.

"I saw a grandmother with two twin boys," he said. "She was my last patient of the day. Those two raced around nonstop, as cute as could be. I remembered what it was like for us."

"It would be hard not to. Jack and Grayson were adorable."

"A handful," he reminded her.

"Yes, but adorable." On that they both agreed. "It took all the energy I had just to keep up with them."

"I think my patient would have said the same. I could see how tired she was."

"I can relate. And we had two sets of them." Not that they weren't blessings, she thought. "I've been thinking a lot about old times, when the kids were small."

"Me, too." His gait stopped.

So did hers. The noise of the tree lot and the town street faded into silence. It felt as if they were alone together. Emotions tangled up inside until she couldn't breathe. As if he felt the same way, Brian moved in closer until he was all she could see. His hand cradled the side of her face, and she could not stop the wish rising up from her soul. The wish to spend more time with him. The wish for there to be more than polite banter between them.

"Do you remember the way it used to be with us?" he whispered.

"Before the twins came along?" The words sounded as besotted as she felt, as hopeful as she felt.

"We were so close," Brian remembered, his

voice husky with affection. "You breathed, I breathed. Your heart beat, my heart beat. I thought we were soul mates."

"I did, too." The earth felt unsteady beneath her, so she clutched Brian's muscled arm with her free hand, holding on tight. She was in danger of falling in love with him again. "Are you going to kiss me?"

"I'm thinking about it." His gaze roved over her face and focused on her lips. "I'm trying to think of a reason why I shouldn't."

"Me, too, but I can't come up with a single one." Mostly because her brain refused to work. There was only feeling, pure feeling. Powerful affection ebbed into the broken places in her heart, the places shattered by their failed marriage. "This isn't sensible."

"Or smart. But I still want to kiss you."

"I still want you to."

Neither of them moved, but the air between them filled with sweet longing. She drew in a shaky breath, gripping the wool sleeve of his coat. Her heart opened again, vulnerable and defenseless, and she couldn't stop it. It was frightening to think that he might kiss her. He might want to get closer. Terror thudded through her, but she didn't move away.

"Hey, boss!" Emmett, one of the stable boys, swaggered up with a girl at his side.

Belle released her hold on Brian's sleeve and reared back, blushing. Rumors would be flying. First the encounter in the kitchen, and now this. "Hi, Emmett and Carolyn."

"Hi, Belle." Carolyn helped Lupita after school a few afternoons a week and lent an extra hand whenever it was needed. The teenager tossed her shiny black hair behind her shoulder. A lovely girl, sweet and vivacious, although tonight she looked unusually pale. "Are you picking out your tree? That's why we're here, too."

"For Carolyn and her mom," Emmett said. "My folks go artificial when it comes to trees."

"Emmett's being awesome and treating me to a real tree," Carolyn explained, beaming at her boyfriend. "My budget's pretty tight."

"That's nice of you." Belle thought well of the young man, too, who worked to help support his family. He was a fine teenager with a great work ethic. He'd worked for them for almost a year now. "Christmas isn't the same without a tree. Come look around with us."

"Okay." Carolyn smiled wanly, Emmett nodded and the four of them headed down the row. "I'm glad you're out of the convalescent center. My mom and I stopped by Ranchland Manor a few times, but you were in a coma."

"I didn't know you'd been by. Thank you." Belle couldn't help being touched by that. Brian's arm brushed her shoulder as they walked. He stayed a whisper away, his dark gaze intent on her, studying her as if he were still debating the merits of kissing her. "I was wondering if you could help us with our holiday baking tomorrow. If you would like to work, we'd love to have you help."

"Yes, I'm so there." Carolyn lit up, as charming as could be. It was impossible not to be fond of Lupita's kindhearted niece. "I could really use the extra hours. Got Christmas presents to buy, you know?"

"I do. Then we'll see you bright and early in the morning." She saw the twins and Carter ahead, huddled in a group, debating the merits of an eight-foot tree, which appeared to be the best on the lot.

"That's more our price range over there," Emmett said, gesturing toward the far corner. "I'll see you tomorrow—I'm on the early shift in the barn. Dr. Wallace, I hear Jack has threatened to take you riding."

"Let's pray he doesn't make good on the threat," Brian teased. "You kids have a nice evening."

"I keep trying to get them interested in church," Belle admitted after they were out of hearing range. "Trying, but not succeeding."

"Knowing you, you'll succeed." Brian's hand

crept into hers and held on. "Do you fall in love with everyone you come across?"

"I can't help it," she quipped with his dark eyes on hers, intent, as if he could see everything.

"Mom and Dad, we're unanimous," Jack called out to them. "Unless you two have dissenting votes?"

"Not me," Brian answered in his good-natured way.

"I wouldn't dream of it," Belle answered. "Remember the last time we were all tree hunting together?"

"I bought a twelve-dollar scrub of a pine. The boys were toddlers."

"Yes, and Maddie and Violet were babies." It no longer hurt to remember that bittersweet time before divorce—and unspeakable danger—tore their family apart. "We had a good time that night. The boys decorated."

"Not what I'd call it. Tossing the ornaments on the floor to watch them roll isn't decorating." Brian laughed. "I'd better go help Jack."

"He doesn't need it. Look at him and Grayson and Carter. They can manhandle the tree. You can't fool me. You're going to go pay for it."

"I'm still the dad around here. I get to pay." He stepped away, but she couldn't. She stayed frozen in place, unable to blink. Although he'd left her side, he felt closer to her than ever.

It felt just like old times, but better.

Chapter Eleven

"Put it right here." Violet led the way through the living room to the corner, where Maddie set a tree stand into position. "Careful of the picture on the wall."

"This is a bigger tree than last year," Jack said from behind thick evergreen boughs. The fir's rich scent tinged the air, mixing with the aroma of the beef stew Lupita had simmering on the stove.

Belle felt useless sitting in a nearby corner, but even she had to admit she couldn't help wrestle the big tree into the house, not in her condition. She could supervise, however. "A little to the left, guys."

"I know, I know," Jack said with impertinent mirth. "You don't always have to be in charge, right?"

"I don't mind it, Mom." Grayson winked as

he tightened his grip around the top of the tree and arrowed it toward Maddie.

"Around the couch," she reminded him, ducking just in time. "Not over."

"Sorry, can't see where I'm going," Carter quipped, good-naturedly peering over the thick limbs toward the tree's base.

"We always do artificial at my house," Brian admitted, lugging the tree's thick trunk. "I never have time for the real thing."

"No kidding," Maddie spoke up. "Not that I minded, let's face it. Decorating was simple. Dad always gets the pre-lit trees, so it's just a matter of taking it out of the box."

"It's up in a snap," Grayson agreed as he heaved along with everyone else, standing the regal fir upright. "But it doesn't smell like this. This is the scent of Christmas."

"I could get used to this." Carter knelt alongside Brian and helped work the trunk into the holder. "Belle, you know how to do Christmas right."

"And don't you forget it." Christmas had never felt so full of promise before.

"Maddie, dear, could you fetch some water for the tree?" Brian asked from beneath the branches. He looked so *right* at the center with their children encircling him that Belle had to turn away.

Trying to hide her reaction, she opened the huge plastic bins Jack and Carter had brought out from storage and sorted through the ornaments. Crystal caught the light as she lifted handblown candy canes and icicles, and laid them carefully on the coffee table. Behind her the kids talked, Brian answered and the familiar notes of his voice touched her like a dream.

"These are fancy." Suddenly he was beside her. "A long way from the ones on our first Christmas tree, remember?"

"Are you telling me you remember cutting strips of construction paper to make into a garland chain?" They'd been sixteen, nearly married, cozy in their tiny rental.

"How many times did I poke myself with a needle stringing popcorn?" He ran a fingertip over the curve of the glass candy cane. "It had to be a couple dozen times."

"You were terrible with a needle and thread."

"But I got better as I went. Later on, it gave me a head start when I learned to suture." Pleasant crinkles gathered in the corners of his eyes. "We made paper snowflakes for ornaments."

"I couldn't believe how fast you could cut them out. Snip, snip, snip, and you were done when I was struggling."

"Since you could string popcorn faster, I'd say we came out even."

"We made a lovely first Christmas together back then." Hope, small and faint, twinkled to life within her. It was foolish to wish for another chance with Brian. "I hope the twins can do that this year. This will be their only chance. Next year there will be weddings and births to celebrate."

"Which means they will have their own family traditions to begin," Brian finished, his gaze locked on hers, speaking the words in her thoughts. "Our kids will be celebrating their own firsts from here on out. It's a blessing from above that we are all here together this Christmas."

"Yes, it is." For a second, her wish didn't seem far-fetched. Brian's hand covered hers with a shock of connection, and she felt the wish within her strengthen.

"I'll get the lights," a voice behind her said, and Violet charged up, beautiful and bright. "Mom, Dad, you two aren't making very much progress unpacking the ornaments."

"Just talking," Belle explained before Violet could read more into the moment, as she'd done last night.

"Right, we'll get to work." Brian veered around the side of the coffee table, putting room between them, and started digging out ornaments.

While Jack and Grayson strung lights, Carter, Violet and Maddie supervised, handing out suggestions and cheerful chatter. A fire crackled in the hearth, Lupita put instrumental Christmas music on in the background and the scent of beef stew trailed in from the kitchen. Brian worked near her in companionable silence. Their fingers occasionally brushed as they reached for the same ornament. She hadn't been this happy since she was sixteen.

Belle. He couldn't take his attention off her. All through the tree decorating, he'd been aware of her presence and every breath she took. As hard as he tried to concentrate on anything else, she remained at the edges of his mind. His will wasn't strong enough, he feared nothing was. All he wanted was to be near her, to see her smile, listen to her gentle alto and long for the music of her laughter. But it was after supper and well into the evening and the kids had her attention.

All he could do was watch from his place by the fire. He admired the natural accord she had with the twins and the way she drew Carter in and made him belong. She stood in the light of the Christmas tree, offering advice on the final touches, watched as Violet moved an ornament here or there, and nodded as Maddie adjusted a length of crystal garland. Belle had only become more gorgeous over the years. She wore a simple cabled sweater and worn jeans, but she was a vision. The jeweled Christmas tree lights brought out the red tones in her auburn hair and basked her in a soft glow.

Simply watching her filled him with sheer contentment. It was time to face facts. *Like* was too weak a word to describe his feelings. What he felt was new and powerful, stronger than before. Falling for her had been easy. Tonight he'd felt relaxed with her, sharing easy conversation at the dinner table and watching their grown children trim the tree. The mistakes he'd made in his past weighed on him, keeping him from laying a hand on her shoulder or leaning in to whisper in her ear or kissing her when he'd had the chance.

"I made your favorite." Belle scooted toward him, two mugs clutched by their handles in one hand. "Eggnog lattes."

"Smells delicious." Rich and creamy with a hint of coffee, he breathed in the aroma as he accepted a cup. "Shouldn't you be off your feet? Let me think what the doctor's orders were—"

"Stop, you know exactly what they were, and I'm just fine." Glittering as brightly as the Christmas tree, Belle eased onto the couch beside him. "I'm glad you stayed. I'm glad you're here."

"Good to know you changed your mind on wanting me out." He winked at her and took a sip of his steaming drink. Tasty, but hot.

"It wasn't that I didn't want you. I just didn't

want you so close." She blushed a little. "I know that doesn't seem like it makes sense."

"It makes perfect sense. You look at me and you can't help but remember how much I let you down."

"Brian, it wasn't like that. I let you down." Her face etched with pain, she stared into her cup. "I really don't want to go there. Not this evening when it's been so wonderful between us."

"You're right. There's no sense in trying to resolve it." His heart took a hit, but he'd known all along it was coming. Tonight was a treasure, getting to be with her. It wasn't how his life would always go. Belle couldn't be his future, not after their past. "The kids are happy."

"Ecstatic." But she didn't look across the room at their children. When she raised her gaze from her cup, it was his face she focused on. "What I meant was, I feared that having you here would be painful. That it would be a constant reminder of our unhappy times."

"When we fought?"

"And the nights I cried myself to sleep." A hint of that old pain surfaced, honest in her unguarded gaze.

"I didn't know, Belle." He swallowed hard, ashamed he hadn't realized how truly unhappy he'd made his wife.

"How could you have known? You were at

work. Remember you had three jobs that summer?" Her hand rested on his forearm. "But things have changed. The danger has finally passed, and having you here has been great for the twins. It reminds Carter that he is a rightful part of this family, as your son. And we're making good memories together again, for their sake."

Her words hooked him and there was no escape. He wished for a chance with Belle with all his heart. "This feels right, doesn't it?"

"Yes, and getting along with you feels right, too." She watched him intently with the smallest twist of emotion soft on her dear face. Was that hope she felt? Was it caring?

Overcome, he tried to speak and couldn't. He cleared his throat. "I'd like to think we can be friends again."

"After all, that's how it started between us." She cast her gaze downward. "It's how it should be now."

Had that been a wish in her eyes or just nostalgia?

"I agree," he said. *Friends.* It was so much less than what he wanted; so much more than he deserved. He took a sip of latte, let the eggnog sweetness roll across his tongue and realized he'd never felt more content. All these years, happiness had eluded him. Now he knew why. It was Belle. She'd been the reason he hadn't felt whole in twenty-five years.

"Mom's finally asleep," Violet reported, slipping into Carter's room and closing the door. "Or at least, she should be by now. Her light is off."

"And Dad is tucked downstairs watching late-night television." Grayson offered his sister a chair and took the floor. "We should be all right as long as Mom and Dad don't decide to meet in the kitchen again."

"Can you believe Dad's eye? It's as black as could be, poor guy." Maddie shook her head. "I wish I'd had a front row seat to what was really going on."

"I came in too late to be sure, but there was something there, if you ask me." Carter crossed his arms over his broad chest, confident of his assessment.

"Mom and Dad seemed close tonight. Did you notice?" Violet smiled at her twin, who easily finished her thought.

"The quiet looks, the little smiles, the way Dad couldn't stop watching her." Maddie nodded.

"I'm just glad they are getting along," Jack spoke from the corner, a little too roughly. "Mom doesn't need any upset. She's doing well with her recovery, her color is good and so is her strength. I'm going to take her outside tomorrow."

"Don't let her do any work," Grayson argued.

"No, I'll let her look around, breathe in the fresh air and be with the animals. I know she misses her horse." Jack understood his mother. He knew feeling a part of this land was vital to who she was, and it would make a difference in her healing. "As soon as she's better, we can talk to her about the rumors."

"I'm starting to really dislike those rumors." Maddie scrunched up her face unhappily. "Mostly because they stayed at the back of my mind tonight. We were having so much fun decorating the tree, but whenever I saw Mom and Dad together, I thought, is the rumor true? Is that the reason they couldn't make their marriage work? Was the truth just too much of a strain?"

"We don't know what the truth is, that's the problem," Grayson said matter-of-factly as he gave his twin a pointed look. "Is Joe Earl our real father? The only one who knows for sure is Mom."

"That's not entirely true," Carter interjected. "There's someone else."

"Who?" Violet asked.

"Dad." Carter launched off the foot of the bed, his boots hitting the floor. "I say we talk to him and put this to a rest. Jack and Grayson, this can't be easy for you after tonight."

"The more time I spend with Dad, the more I

want him to be my real father." Jack pushed off the wall where he'd been leaning. "I agree. Let's talk to him. What do you think, Gray?"

"I just want to know. All these years, there was no doubt in my mind, but now I look at my father and this eats at me. What if he's been keeping a secret this whole time?" Grayson stood and steeled his shoulders. "I say we ask him. Maddie?"

"I vote yes." Maddie stood, as well.

Violet jumped to her feet. "I'll make it unanimous."

They spilled into the hallway, quiet so as not to wake their mom. The space beneath her door stayed dark, no light flicked on as they padded by the master suite and descended the stairs. Anxiety jumped in Jack's chest. This was the moment of truth, he thought, as he led the way through the dark house, following the faint glow from the TV.

"Hey, gang. What's up?" Brian removed the ice pack from his eye. The swelling was gone and the purple-black color was fading to a lighter purple. "I thought you were all heading up to bed."

"We were, but we have something on our minds." Jack eased into the chair across from him while the others filled in a semicircle around Brian, taking couch cushions and chairs. He leaned forward and hit Pause, freezing the broadcast image in place. "We'd like to talk. Do you mind?"

"No. I'm here whenever you kids need it." Brian set the ice pack on the coffee table, concern furrowing his brow. "Whatever this is, it looks serious."

"Unfortunately." Grayson cleared his throat. "You know we were at a loss when you'd gone missing and Belle was in her coma. We'd found each other, we discovered we were separated twins, but we still didn't know why."

"Until you and Mom told us about David Johnson and the Witness Protection Program," Maddie piped in.

"What we didn't tell you—" Violet began.

"Is that we did an investigation of our own," Maddie finished.

"We tracked down the Fort Worth address where you and Belle first lived," Carter explained. "We tried to put as many pieces together as we could."

"We talked to Patty Earl," Maddie said gently.

"Patty Earl?" Brian shook his head. "I haven't heard that name in a long time. How did you find her?"

"It was me." Violet's gaze turned apologetic. "I found an old picture with you, Mom and all four of us when we were very small. There was a house number in the background."

"So we went down there," Jack continued. "Patty Earl still lived across the street, and she told us you weren't our father. That her deceased husband, Joe, was."

Brian rubbed a hand over his face. He couldn't believe what they were telling him. All these years he hadn't given a thought to that part of his past. He blew out a breath. "I'm sorry you kids had to hear all that. How long have you been dealing with it?"

"Since not long after Mom went into a coma," Violet answered. "We were blown away by Patty Earl's insinuations."

"So we had DNA tests taken." Jack pulled an envelope out of his back pocket and set it on the coffee table.

Grayson did the same. "We needed answers, Dad."

"And you couldn't ask your mother, of course." Brian leaned back against the cushion, a little shell-shocked.

"We're still afraid to," Maddie confessed.

"We don't want to hurt her," Violet explained. "The rumors aren't pretty, and it implies some terrible things about her. That Mom was sleeping around when she was in high school. That she lied and tricked you. I know neither of you were Christians then, but Mom is such a good person. It's hard to believe she would have behaved so badly and then lied about you and all because she wanted to marry into a rich family."

"Those *are* ugly rumors." He took a moment, let a beat pass, more troubled than he could say. "I'd hoped those rumors were buried forever. I thought I'd finally left them behind, and here they are again. All through our marriage, it's all we heard. How Belle duped me, saying I was Jack and Grayson's father when I wasn't. I can't tell you the strain it put on us."

Five faces watched him, riveted, silently waiting for the answer to the question they had been asking for the better part of six months.

"I never, ever, believed Patty." He said it in no uncertain terms, so they could hear the truth boom in his voice. He wanted no doubts about this. "I know in my heart you boys are my sons."

"But why would Patty Earl say such a thing?" Maddie asked.

"And how did the rumors get started?" Violet looked as if she feared that such pervasive lies had to have a grain of truth in them.

Just like everyone else at the time, Brian thought sadly. He knew how convincing Patty and her husband could be. "Joe Earl and I were rivals in high school, especially when he was sure he'd be captain of the football team and I ended up with it. That was the breaking point. He had never wanted to get along with me, but that's when dislike turned to hatred." He sighed. "I felt sorry for Joe, and I still do. He was full of hate, he had no faith, he wasn't happy. Maybe he had problems at home. But he did his best to make my life miserable. I didn't know he had a crush on Belle until she and I had started dating."

"But did Mom ever date Joe?" Jack asked.

"No, never. He wanted her for his own. He made no secret of that. When Belle found herself pregnant, I proposed and we married quickly. That's when the rumors started." He would never forget how that vicious gossip wounded his new bride. "Pretty soon everyone we knew had heard them. I think Joe told it so well and often, even he started to believe himself."

"But you never did." Grayson said it as if he wanted to be clear, as if he needed to hear it one more time.

"Never. Not for a single minute." Brian took the time to look each twin in the eye. "I had no doubt. Not in twenty-seven years."

A movement caught the edge of his vision. He felt a brush against his soul and he knew who it was before she stepped into the light. Belle.

"Mom! You're up." Maddie looked worried.

"I hope not for very long," Violet said, a little guiltily.

"I've been here long enough and I couldn't help overhearing." Belle crossed into the room, the hem of her pretty bathrobe swirling with her steps.

"Come sit with me." Brian rose and held out his hand to bring her to him. When she laid her palm over his, it felt *right,* as if God had scripted this moment just for them. He helped her ease onto the couch, and when she let go of his hand, his heart just kept falling. Just for a moment, it didn't feel wrong to dream.

Chapter Twelve

"I'm sorry I wasn't able to talk to you about this before. I didn't know you kids knew about the rumors." Belle felt miserable thinking of what her children had been wrestling with on their own. "That's a lot to keep inside."

"Us?" Maddie shook her head. "But we're—"

"—more worried about you," Violet assured her.

Jack's tone vibrated with resolve. "We love you, Mom."

"That's never been in question," Grayson announced.

"I love you kids so much. All of you." Even though Carter wasn't her child by blood, he was hers by heart. "I'm thankful you brought this up with your father, because Brian *is* your father."

Silent relief swept through the room at the words. Her sons looked relieved, but her attention stayed riveted on the man at her side. She was aware of the firm press of his knee to hers and the iron muscles of his arm against her shoulder as they sat side by side. Together.

"Brian has been the only man in my life. *Ever*." The old rumors still caused a harsh jolt of pain. The accusations she feared Brian just might have believed down deep, even if he hadn't wanted to believe them. Hadn't that been one of the stresses on their marriage? The rumors hadn't died, they'd persisted—whispered behind her in line at the grocery store or when she was at the park with the boys, holding Brian's hand.

"Jack, Grayson." She faced her sons, needing to put the insinuations to rest for good. "No one else could possibly be your father. I know Patty Earl was convincing, believe me. I had to endure the fervor of those vicious rumors, but she and Joe were two of a kind. She was jealous that I was with Brian—I think she had a big crush on him and she lashed out with her jealousy. She helped spread the gossip as if it was her personal mission. You know how high school pettiness can be."

"But it's over now." Brian's hand closed over hers. "I hope you can put the rumors to rest, too."

"You answered our questions." Maddie swiped her eyes. "I'm sorry, I'm just so overcome. Patty and Joe Earl…did they break up your marriage?"

"It played a role." Belle hated to admit it. "We had other problems, but it was—"

"—a wound between us," Brian finished for her, finding the words she could not. "It made Belle look like a terrible woman."

"And down deep, I always worried you feared it was true." There. She'd said it. The truth was out, and she felt lighter.

"Not for one single second," he assured her, squeezing her hand. "I know the woman you are, Belle. I never doubted you. I've always believed in you."

Relief and joy caught in her throat. His words meant everything. Brian was the best man she knew, who did what was right and true. He'd stood beside her and believed in her all this time, and she'd never realized. She saw him through new eyes.

"I believe you, too." Jack's voice sounded strained and emotion twisted his face. "I know the truth in my heart."

"Me, too." Grayson nodded, his gruff tone layered with feeling.

"We finally know what happened." Maddie brushed away a final tear. "The mystery is solved."

"I'm so sorry those rumors hurt you," Violet said gently. "It's worse that we brought them up again, fearing they were true."

"It's all right, I understand." Brian spoke up, clearing his throat. The old Brian would have been clipped, closed off, logical. But he'd changed. Grace shone in his eyes like unshed tears. "I know why you doubted me. It's because I wasn't entirely truthful with Grayson and Maddie to begin with."

"If this is about Sharla—" Grayson started.

"We understand," Maddie finished while Carter nodded sympathetically beside her. "You wanted to keep Mom, Jack and Violet safe."

"I never corrected your assumption that Sharla was your real mother, when she wasn't." Brian faced Maddie and Grayson. "I'm sorry, but also I wanted to spare you more pain. You'd lost your real mother to witness protection. I couldn't bear to divulge the truth when you'd lost the only mother you knew. Can you forgive me?"

"It's already done," Grayson assured him, while Maddie nodded in agreement.

"I still want you to think of Sharla as your mom, too." What had once been a wound to her soul was gone. Belle took Brian's hand in both of her own. "She was a good mother to you, that's plain to see. She loved you, and you loved her. She should never be forgotten."

"Thanks." Grayson's single nod spoke volumes.

As Maddie blinked at her through teary eyes,

Belle felt Brian's grip tighten. When she met his gaze, she read what words could never express.

"Thanks for telling us everything." Jack was the first to stand. When his arms wrapped around Belle and held her close, she sensed something deeper than his forgiveness. His acceptance. The issue that had always stood between them had been healed.

"It feels good to have this wrapped up." Grayson shouldered in to hug Belle. "It means a lot."

"Good night, you two." Maddie squeezed in next. "The question of our past is behind us. We can all move forward now."

"Something tells me our futures will be bright." Violet kissed Belle's cheek. "We're together again, and we're going to stay that way."

"Just try and get rid of me," Maddie quipped, as the girls linked arms and followed their older brothers from the room.

"Come here, Carter." Belle held out her arms, giving him a hug. "I know I can never replace your mother, but I hope you can think of me as family."

"I already do." Carter kissed her cheek, too, before hugging his father good-night. Love filled the air as he joined his siblings. "Hey, what about the DNA results?"

"We don't need to open the envelopes," Jack

and Grayson answered in unison. "Good night, Mom and Dad."

"Good night." Brian watched his children leave the room, feeling strangely light. He picked up the official-looking envelopes thoughtfully and set them on the mantel. "Well, that was unexpected."

"And illuminating." She moved toward him, graceful even with her bum leg. The light found the luster in her hair and made her ivory complexion luminescent. Her dark eyes were radiant as she joined him in front of the fire. "I never knew you felt that way about me."

"I wasn't good at saying a lot of things back then, especially what was closest to my heart." He couldn't tear his gaze away from her, his pulse drumming in his veins because he was afraid he was the one dreaming. "You were always closest to my heart, Belle."

"As you were to mine. I see now why you remarried. Because you had to go on with your life for the children's sake."

"If there had been a hope of being with you again—" He was in danger of saying too much. "But there wasn't any. When I met Sharla, she was kind and loving and the kids took to her. I loved her."

"I know." Tears stood in her eyes. "Look at us getting along."

"We aren't arguing." He smiled, too, fighting the pull of dreams he wanted to give in to. "Have you looked up?"

"Mistletoe." She cast her gaze at the ceiling above. "Do you know what this means?"

"I do. It's tradition." He moved in, closer, until their breaths mingled. "I don't have any choice."

"No, you don't."

"I have to kiss you." His lips grazed hers.

"Yes, you do." She said no more as his mouth slanted over hers with a kiss so tender, time stood still. For one moment, he knew perfection. Her velvet-soft lips, her sweet kiss, the feel of her in his arms. Love filled his heart and stayed, even when she moved away.

"Sleep well." She gripped her cane and ambled from him, taking his entire heart.

He had nothing left. Everything he was, and would ever be, would be hers.

"Mom, you've been especially happy this morning." A cheerful voice penetrated her thoughts.

"Happy?" She set the sprinkler shaker on the counter and blinked, bringing the kitchen into focus along with her beautiful daughters. "Why wouldn't I be?"

"She looked a million miles away, didn't she?" Violet asked her twin.

"She surely did," Maddie agreed. "The question is, what could possibly put that blissful look on her face?"

"Or who?" Violet smiled. "I know that I only get that goofy look when I'm daydreaming about Landon."

"Now that you mention it, I probably act the same way after date night with my fella," Maddie piped in. "So what gives, Mom?"

"Isn't being here with you two enough?" *Good save, Belle,* she told herself. If the girls knew about last night's kiss, then she would never hear the end of it. "Here we are making Christmas cookies."

"*Hundreds* of Christmas cookies," Violet corrected.

"God bless Lupita for mixing up all the dough ahead of time." Maddie grabbed the last chunk from the refrigerator and set it on the counter to roll. "I love you, Lupita."

"She's off today and can't hear you." Belle shook red and green sprinkles over the iced cookies spread out before her in rows of cooling racks. "We're lost without her, but we're thankful for you, Carolyn."

"I do what I can." The teenager swirled a spatula in the frosting bowl and swiped icing carefully over a sugar cookie. "Thanks for having me in to work today. I love making cookies."

"And we need the extra help." Pleased to have

found an excuse to give Carolyn the chance to earn extra Christmas wages, Belle set down her shaker and picked up a bag of small candies. "Do you know what we need to do this week?"

"What *don't* we need to do this week?" Violet answered. "We still have to get the house lights up, but we need to buy new ones. Last year's are toast."

"I vote icicle lights," Maddie chimed in.

"Me, too," Carolyn seconded, looking unusually pale as she frosted a cookie. "Not that I have a vote, but I have an opinion."

"And it's a good one," Belle assured her. "We'll make it unanimous. Icicle lights. There are the garlands to get up along the banisters and the stockings on the mantel."

"And Christmas shopping." Maddie sprinkled flour on the pastry mat and grabbed her rolling pin. "I'm way behind."

"Me, too," Violet agreed.

"I haven't even started." Belle pressed colorful candies shaped like ornaments into the Christmas tree cookie. "Of course, I had a really good excuse."

"Coma," the twins said together, rolling their eyes. "That's like the worst excuse."

"No kidding. I've got to hit the stores running." Belle moved on to another cookie. "Our family has grown since we were here last. I'll need suggestions for Landon, Violet. Maddie, I already have a couple of ideas for Ty and his daughter. And that's just the start of my list."

"We haven't discussed how we're doing Christmas this year." Maddie set down her rolling pin. "I was hoping to spend the day with Ty and Darcy."

"And I want to be with Landon," Violet confessed.

"I'm sure the boys feel the same way. We have Elise and her son, Keira and Savannah." Belle knew exactly what she wanted. This house brimming full of family and togetherness and hope for the future. "We'll invite everyone here for Christmas Eve dinner to stay the night. We'll catch the candlelight service and spend Christmas day right here, celebrating the day the way it ought to be. What do you think?"

"Perfect." Violet's eyes misted. "We'll be together, all of us—"

"For Christmas," Maddie finished. "I'll let the boys know. We'll get it set up, Mom."

"We are going to have a lot of stockings to fill, but first, we'd better get these cookies done." Tears of gratitude stung Belle's eyes. She picked up the shaker and sprinkled the star-shaped cookies Carolyn was frosting. "We have to box most of these up for gifts. I haven't even started a list. There's Jeb, our minister. The ladies at

Ranchland Manor and the nurses. My physical therapist."

"And Doc Garth," Violet suggested. "Oh, and our neighbors, as usual."

"And Sadie." Maddie dusted a cookie cutter with flour and plunged it into the dough. "We can't forget her."

"She's such a dear," Violet agreed.

"It's a good thing Aunt Lupita had me pick up a lot of gift boxes." Carolyn set down her bowl, moving slowly. Perhaps the poor girl was coming down with something. "I'll get them folded up, unless you need me to do other stuff, Belle?"

"No, sounds perfect." Her gaze drifted to the window and joy crept into her soul. Brian stood in the yard, bundled in a winter coat. Jack must have found an extra Stetson for his father to wear, as the men had been repairing a downed fence this morning. All three sons surrounded Brian, talking away. Seeing him reminded her of their kiss.

Heat flushed her face, a telltale sign she didn't want the girls figuring out. As if he felt her gaze, Brian glanced her way. He spotted her, nodded once in recognition and smiled slow and true, capturing another piece of her heart.

The boys turned to see where he was looking, saw her in the window and waved. Jack launched forward, hiking toward the house with his long-legged stride. Perhaps he had business he needed to talk about with her regarding the barn or the animals, so she wiped her hands on a dish towel, left Violet to finish the decorating and headed toward the back door to meet him.

Jack wasn't there alone. Brian was with him, dazzling her. He looked manly in a Stetson and cowboy boots, holding open the door for her. Her tongue tied as she reached for her coat. Her fingers fumbled with the buttons. What was wrong with her?

"It's warming up out here," Jack explained. "Guess it's okay for you to come outside now."

"We didn't want you getting too cold." Brian took her cane from her, allowing her to finish buttoning with ease. "You know the doctor's orders. No riding."

"Right. And when he gives the okay, I have to wear a special helmet." She pulled her gloves out of her coat pockets. "But I get to see Mouse?"

"Finally," Brian confirmed with a slow smile.

Excitement surged through her. It was a long walk to the horse barn, and the round trip was more than her leg would have tolerated before this. "I'm ready. Give me my cane and let's go."

"I figured you'd be rearin' to go." Brian handed it over to her. "You were getting around pretty good yesterday."

"I was hoping to get around the barn next."

He laughed, bringing lines to the corners of his eyes. Their gazes met and visions of last night's kiss danced into her thoughts. Sweet, sweet, sweet.

Brian's cell chose that moment to ring. He tugged it out of his pocket and when he glanced at the screen, his forehead furrowed. "Not sure, but this could be a patient. I gave out my number to several this week. I should take this."

"Sure. We'll go ahead and you can catch up with us," she said. He flashed her an apologetic look before taking the call.

She accompanied Jack down the stairs and breathed in the fresh, wintry air. With the Texas land at her feet and the Texas sky above, she felt whole again. She'd looked forward to this moment since she'd first opened her eyes in the convalescent centre, craving the open feel of endless plains and distant horizons, but as complete as she felt, it wasn't enough. Not anymore.

Brian's voice drifted over to her, and she knew why. She needed him. If she kept wanting to be with him, she was going to get hurt. He would break her heart. But that didn't stop her from turning to watch him talk with his patient, intent on the conversation. Affection filled her up, soul deep.

"Sorry, I've got to go." Brian ended the call, clutched his phone in his hand and sprinted over to her. "I wanted to spend time with you, Belle, but the grandmother I saw yesterday has taken a turn for the worse. Pneumonia is tricky, and I need to admit her to the hospital. She has no insurance, so she needs someone to fight for her."

"There's no one better than you." *Proud* was too small a word for what she felt for this man. "I understand. Go. Keep us updated, okay?"

"Thanks, Belle." His hand squeezed hers. It felt as if they belonged together. The broken pieces and old wounds in her heart began to fill with the light of love. No longer dark, no longer hurting, they glowed brightly with hope as Brian released her and walked away. But no matter how far he went, there was no distance between them.

She watched him go with wishes whispering in her soul and dreams she was afraid to dream.

Although it was only afternoon, Brian felt as if it were midnight. He'd spent several trying hours at the closest hospital, an hour away, getting Allie admitted and settled. The grandmother's condition had deteriorated overnight because she hadn't followed his orders, and he feared for her. He left her in the care of a fine specialist, but worry stuck with him. He had a bad feeling about it.

On the drive back to Grasslands, the only thing that could force his thoughts from his ill patient was Belle. She'd been radiant this morning, beautiful from the inside out. Her flawless ivory complexion, her exquisite face, her innate kindness, all overwhelmed him. Worse, he could still feel the impression of her hand tucked in his. He stared at the rolling ribbon of road ahead of him and couldn't wait to get back to her.

And maybe kiss her again. Remembering the way he'd held her in his arms and the sweet brush of her lips made him ache with disappointment too strong to bear. He didn't deserve her. He'd destroyed any chance of deserving her when he'd kept his heart closed, made her miserable, and she had asked him for a separation.

The darkening skies cast a grim foreboding across the land as he pulled into the long gravel driveway of the Colby Ranch. Windows gleamed in the gloom, cheerful and welcoming and tempting him to think of home. For one brief instant, he remembered being married to Belle, bringing a surprise dinner for just the two of them—a coupon special from the local pizza joint—and a handful of daisies he'd picked in a roadside field.

He recalled the anticipation he'd felt and how she'd heard the car in the driveway and flung open the front door of their little rental on Riley Street. She'd been beautiful with her auburn hair spilling over her shoulders like liquid bronze. She'd laid a hand on her pregnant belly, obvious beneath the flowery sundress she wore. She'd flown down the walk in her bare feet, his beautiful bride. He'd never forget the punch of love so strong it blinded him as he'd handed her the daisies. When he'd kissed her, it had been with all the devotion in his soul.

That's what he'd destroyed. Weary, he pulled into a parking spot next to the garage and turned off the engine. The guilt and grief remained so deep he couldn't rise out of the mire. He didn't know how long he sat in the twilight. A knock on the window startled him.

"Are you okay?" Belle stared in at him, bundled in her wool coat, with a knit cap on her head. Her auburn hair spilled out to frame her face, which reminded him of when he'd given her daisies and they'd shared a pizza over conversation and laughter. Could it be that way again?

He didn't know. Agony tore through him as he pulled out his key and opened the door. "I just have a lot on my mind."

"How is your patient?" she asked.

"Very grim. Some forms of pneumonia are very aggressive." He was also reminded of his recent battle with strep, a battle he'd nearly lost. "She's getting the best care, but I fear she underplayed her symptoms when I saw her yesterday, and after that, she didn't take care of herself."

"Brian, I'm so sorry." Compassion softened

ier features, made her too alluring to resist. Love ind longing filled him, dreams for what could iot be.

He didn't deserve a second chance, even as ie prayed for it.

"At least she's getting the treatment she needs iow." He drew in a shaky breath. "How was your rip to the barn?"

"Sustaining. It was just what I needed to feel ike myself again."

"You look amazing." The truth slipped out, vords he'd be smart to hold back. "I've never een you like this. Luminous."

"Maybe having you around is good for me, oo." Love. It shone up at him unmistakable and ionest. "Can I ask a favor?"

"Always. Name it." The words felt torn out if him, past the warring guilt and his adoration or her.

"Carolyn is coming down with a flu, I think." Concern marred Belle's forehead. "Maddie has ier lying down. Violet went out to fetch Emmett or her. She's been pretty sick this afternoon."

"She's not lying down now." He gestured to-vard the front porch where the door had opened nd Carolyn emerged, clinging to her boy-riend's hand. Worry marked Emmett's face, ears stained Carolyn's.

"Why aren't you on the couch where Maddie put you?" Belle asked, hurrying toward the young couple. "Carolyn, you're shaking."

"I'm fine, I just need to go home." Carolyn swiped her eyes. "I'm really sorry about leaving before I could help fix supper. I just think that—" She stopped and covered her mouth with her hands.

Nature could not be stopped. The girl headed for the edge of the lawn. Emmett followed her. The clear sound of her being sick echoed in the yard. The first ping of raindrops plopped on the driveway.

"The poor girl." Belle brushed a cool drop off her cheek. "Can you help her, Brian?"

"Sure." He pushed aside his worries to focus on the girl standing up and shakily wiping her mouth on her sleeve.

"I think you should tell them," Emmett said quietly. "We both know what this might be."

"It's not. It's the flu. I just know it," Carolyn argued stubbornly.

That's when Brian knew. He had a flash from his youth, from being that sixteen-year-old boy standing next to his beloved, watching her be sick, feeling her fear and pain and disappointment. It was terrifying to find out that instead of being a teenager, he'd had to grow up overnight.

"Let me see if it's the flu," Brian offered. "It

will take a minute, and if it is, you won't have to worry."

"It's not the flu," Emmett spoke up. "She's—"

"Don't say it!" Carolyn cried out. "Don't, because it's not true. It can't be."

"She told me this morning she's really late," Emmett said, his chest puffing up like a man taking responsibility. "She's been sick three afternoons in a row."

"Not mornings," Carolyn pointed out. "It's called morning sickness, not afternoon sickness."

"Actually, I had afternoon sickness," Belle said quietly. "It sounds to me like maybe we'd better have Violet run into town and pick up a pregnancy test for you."

"It's not that. I'm not p-pregnant," Carolyn insisted, but this time her denial lacked sting. It was the sound of a girl accepting the inevitable.

Chapter Thirteen

Belle slipped into the den, the rhythm of her gait so familiar to him, he didn't need to turn from the window to know it was her. He faced her, wanting to be bathed in her light. He wanted to be free to love her.

"I did everything I could to comfort poor Carolyn." Belle joined him at the window. The storm had come in, hammering down pellets of cold rain from black skies like reality drowning a fool's dream. "She and Emmett are going to tell their families tonight."

"I remember how hard that was." Disgrace still stuck with him. "Facing your parents was the hardest thing I'd done in my young life. They hated me."

"And disowned me." Her hand slid along his arm and held on. "I've never felt so alone, but then I realized I had you. You didn't go anywhere. You stood beside me."

"I tried my best to be there for you."

"I know that." Her hand rested on his shoulder. "I don't know if I ever told you what it meant that you proposed to me that night."

"It was the right thing to do." There he went again, closing up, when he should open his heart. But how did he tell her what was most vulnerable to him? Maybe it was time to do it. He took a breath and gathered his courage. "I loved you so deeply, Belle. There was never a shred of doubt that marrying you was the right thing. No way would I have left you."

"I know. I loved you only the way a first love can be. With everything I had."

"Me, too." He squeezed his eyes shut, fighting not to let her words carry him away. The comfort and connection her touch offered was just one more thing he wasn't worthy to accept. He'd gotten her pregnant. They'd been careful, they'd used protection, but nothing was foolproof and in truth they'd been too young. Too young for the consequences, and if he'd been a Christian then, he would have upheld those values.

"I always feared you hated me down deep," he confessed. "I couldn't be the husband you needed."

"You didn't fail me, Brian." She leaned in, so close he was tempted to draw her into his arms and hold her against his chest where he could keep her safe, where he could trick himself into believing she could be his again.

Lightning cracked across the sky, startling them with a blinding flash. Thunder boomed, rattling the window panes. How did he tell Belle she was wrong? He had broken her heart. There was no way he could hope to win her now.

"I never thanked you for standing by me, Brian." Belle didn't move away. "Going through this with Carolyn, waiting for the pregnancy test results, wondering which way her life would go, reminded me of something. You were a rock when I needed it. You never wavered. You became my husband, my family and the father of our children."

"Then we divorced."

"Well, there was that." Warm, when she should have resented him. "When I look back, there was more love than anything else. I can see that now. I think that's why it hurt so much when things weren't working. We fought hard because it mattered very much."

"Raising a family at such a young age took its toll on us both."

"You're right…it wasn't easy. I just wish I had coped better." There had been days she'd been so overwhelmed, she'd cried. When the boys were sick and up all night, and she'd been ill, too, but the children's needs came first. When they were teething, she walked the floor with both of them while Brian was at work, so exhausted. She loved every minute of it, but they'd had no resources. No help of any kind.

"You were a terrific mom. Don't doubt that for one second, Belle." He leaned in, his words shooting straight to her heart. *Just one more kiss,* she thought, *that's all I need. Just one to remember for always.* But when his lips met hers, it was forever she felt. Forever she wished for. But did he? His lips brushed hers with reverence; it was the kiss of a man who cared beyond words.

When he straightened away, emotion lingered between them.

"I let you down," he said gruffly, scarcely more than a whisper. "I walked out the door when you asked me to. We'd been fighting all night, the boys were sick, the girls were colicky and I'd lost hope. I'll never forgive myself for that. I fear there is no forgiveness."

"Brian, you can't—" That's as far as she got. Maddie breezed into the den with Violet on her heels.

"Oops." Maddie skidded to a stop.

"It looks like we're interrupting, I hope." Violet lifted one eyebrow questioningly.

"What's up, girls?" Brian asked, taking one step away, just one, but his intent was clear. He wanted to put distance between them.

"We were thinking." The girls started in unison, looked at each other and smiled.

"I'll go first," Maddie said. "When we walked Emmett and Carolyn out to his car, Emmett told us he thinks they should get married."

"That's responsible of him." Approval rang in Brian's voice.

"Carolyn doesn't know how they will pay for it all," Violet explained. "She helps support her family, and Emmett helps with his. Emmett is a good employee."

"And Carolyn is Lupita's niece. Maybe it would help them out if we had their wedding here," Maddie suggested. "Not sure what you think, but it's a way to turn this into a positive. To show them they aren't alone. People care about them and want them to do well."

"A wedding." Belle bit her bottom lip. She tried to think but her thoughts stayed focused on Brian. He felt to blame for their unhappiness. Was that the reason he didn't want to move forward? It was impossible to miss the affection in his eyes as he turned to her.

"What do you think?" he asked tenderly, the way a man who loved a woman might. "Remember our wedding?"

"We stood in front of a justice of the peace. It was all we could afford." She heard the quiver of emotion in her words, betraying her, so she said what was in her heart. "Although it wasn't the wedding I'd dreamed of, I wasn't disappointed. I had everything that mattered. You."

"That's how I felt." His voice dipped, betraying him, too. "Like the luckiest man in the world. But I wanted you to have that special day, to walk down the aisle in a beautiful dress and feel the support of all your family and friends."

"That would have mattered." She blinked hard against the sudden rise of tears, remembering how alone she and Brian had been together. Maybe things wouldn't have to be that way for Emmett and Carolyn. She and Brian hadn't been able to save their marriage, but maybe they could make it easier for another young couple. "Let's do it. Let's give them the support they need."

"Excellent!" Maddie beamed, reminding Belle she wasn't in the room alone with Brian.

"We'll give Lupita a call." Violet smiled her approval. "C'mon, Maddie. I think Mom and Dad need to be alone."

"Our beautiful daughters," Belle breathed after the girls hurried from the room and closed the door behind them.

"Yes, they are." Brian traced the line of her jaw with the tip of his finger. "Just like their mother."

Tears filled her eyes because she could sense him moving away from her. Distance stood between them, and she knew it was their talk of the past. Would that always stand between them? And here she'd been hoping for another chance at a happy ending with Brian.

"The boys want me to go out with them again tomorrow morning." Brian's words felt scratchy and sadness rang in the low notes. "I couldn't say no. I had a good time lending a hand with the ranch work this morning, but the early hour is tough."

"Ranching means being up before the sun," Belle agreed, stepping back and giving Brian the distance he wanted. She shored up the disappointment in her heart. After all, he'd made no promises. She'd only been hoping. With all the depth of her soul, but, still, it had been nothing more than hope. "I'll let you get to bed. You're leaving tomorrow, aren't you?"

"After church." He looked strained. Apology carved into the chiseled planes of his face. No man could look more compelling. "I finished my volunteer work at the Grasslands Clinic. I feel as if I can leave now that I've gotten to know Jack and Violet better."

"I understand. You've been away from home for so long." When she wanted to reach out and touch him, to reassure him with a brush of her hand against his, she took another step back. "Remember, you're welcome here anytime."

"I know." Softer emotions enriched his words and gleamed in his eyes that could see straight into her soul. "I'll come for Christmas."

"Christmas Eve dinner, six o'clock. Don't be late." It hurt to smile. It hurt to grasp the doorknob and turn it, knowing he was leaving soon. That he'd never really been hers. He never would be. "I'll text you about the wedding in case you'd like to come."

"I would." He sounded gruff, but sadness filled the air between them. "Good night, Belle."

"Good night." It took all her strength to step across the den's threshold and pull the door shut behind her. She stood alone as thunder rattled the house, and her heart shattered.

He hadn't made the wrong decision. Brian was certain of it, even if sleep had eluded him through the night. He'd tossed and turned and, come morning, it was all he thought about. He was troubled by the look in Belle's eyes as she'd wished him good-night. The sadness there matched his. He had to leave. What other solution was there? Their kisses, their amazing kisses, couldn't be forgotten. Those embraces had been sweet as dreams, full of promise and gentle with love.

Love. That was the one thing he could never let happen, not with Belle. He'd been her husband. He'd been responsible for her happiness. He'd vowed to cherish and honor her and had failed. He'd tried as hard as he knew how, and he'd made her miserable. He had to take responsibility for that.

"Dad, are you sure you have to go?" Violet breezed into the kitchen wearing a pink dress for church, looking as pretty as a rose. "Christmas is almost here. You could stay until then."

"I could." He looked up from the stove, spatula in hand. "But it's time, sweetheart. Remember, I'm always available for you. I'm a phone call or a text message away."

"I know. I'm just glad I got to know you." Tears sparkled in her eyes. "I finally have a dad. I want him around."

"I want to be around," he assured her. "Belle gave me an open invitation, so I may be here so much you'll start hoping I'll leave."

"Not a chance." She circled over to him. "Pancakes?"

"They are Belle's favorite." That choked him up a little, and he prayed it didn't show. "Every Sunday morning, when I wasn't working, I used to make breakfast for your mother. It was one of the few things I could do to honor her. I was always studying or working, and she was running herself ragged with first one set of twins, then two."

"I was thinking about that last night." Maddie sauntered into the kitchen, dressed in blue. "You and Mom got married at sixteen, just like Carolyn and Emmett."

"It's settled, then?" He checked the pancakes, which were bubbling, and flipped them one by one.

"Mom just got a text from Lupita. She said the families had a draining evening discussing things, but the wedding is on." Maddie leaned against the counter at his other side, breathing deep. "I've missed your pancakes, Dad."

"When I couldn't make them for Belle, I made them for you." He kissed her forehead and then Violet's, more grateful than he could say.

"Hey, Dad." Carter loped in, newly showered. Dressed for church, the only thing missing was his tie, which was stuffed into his shirt pocket. "Pancakes. I could smell them coming down the stairs."

"Worked up an appetite keeping up with all of you this morning." He turned the bacon strips sizzling in a fry pan. "Would one of you set the table?"

"I'm on it." Grayson strode in wearing a navy suit, nearly identical to Jack in his black one.

"I'll help," Jack offered, opening a cabinet. Plates clanked together as he hauled them out.

"Dad, you did pretty good this morning. I'll make a cowboy out of you yet."

"I almost have the hang of staying in the saddle," he quipped. The pancakes were golden and perfect, so he flipped them onto a platter. "I could get to like riding a horse."

"Will wonders never cease?" Belle strolled in, cane in hand, looking so gorgeous in dark green silk, she stole every atom of oxygen from his chest. "Brian Wallace, riding a horse? This I have to see."

"It wasn't bad." Somehow he managed to get the words out without a breath of air. "I can see why you like it."

"I love it. We'll all have to go riding sometime—maybe spring. We could make a picnic of it. When I get the doc's okay. What do you think?" Her question really asked something else.

"Sounds good to me." He hoped she could hear the reassurance within his answer. Yes, they could make this work. Yes, they would stay friends for the children's sake. He didn't think he could keep living his life without seeing Belle again. His world was better with her in it, even if it was only a carefully polite arrangement. Something was better than nothing.

They sat down to a family breakfast. Belle said the blessing, reminding him of all he had to be thankful for. The conversation turned merry as they ate. The twins were fun to watch, so alike in many ways and different in others. The boys talked about the ranch, the girls dished about Emmett and Carolyn's wedding and then launched into a discussion about her their upcoming nuptials. He spoke when necessary, but his every sense was tuned to Belle. He wanted to be the man who deserved her, and knowing he wasn't hurt like a mortal wound. Good thing he was leaving for home after the service.

Once the dishes were done, he loaded his bags into the trunk of his car and followed the family caravan to church. Alone in his car, Brian tried not to let thoughts of Belle plague him. He did love her. What he felt for her was not merely renewed love, but different and more substantial. He was no longer that teenage boy. His heart had grown stronger through the years of trial and loss, capable of deeper love. He could not forget the wonder of Belle's kiss or the dream for her he could not let himself pray for.

He pulled into the church lot next to Jack's truck and tucked away his turmoil. His kids were waiting for him. Belle climbed out of Violet's SUV and smiled at him.

Please, Lord, he prayed. *Help me to get through this. I can't do it without You.*

He opened the door and stepped into the crisp

winterlike air, thankful for his family surrounding him. The smiling faces of his kids and their smitten sweethearts. That's what he had to focus on. He fell into stride beside Jack and followed Belle into the church.

Belle listened to Reverend Jeb Miller's sermon with a heavy heart. She stood to sing when the congregation did; she bowed her head to pray when the minister prayed. She tried to keep her mind on the sermon about Mary and Joseph, but Brian kept creeping into her thoughts. Maybe because she could see him out of the corner of her eye on the other side of Violet, earnestly listening to the end of the sermon.

What was wrong with her that she couldn't concentrate? Brian had made it clear. There could be nothing more between them. She had to let her hopes go, but instead she found herself praying. *Isn't there any way You can give us a second chance, Lord?*

Maybe that was asking for the wrong thing, she didn't know. Maybe God had other plans for her and Brian, separately. She rose to sing the final hymn. This was in God's hands and would always be. She had to trust in Him and let it go.

The service ended, the congregation broke into murmurs and worshippers stepped into the aisle.

Time to face Brian. Belle tried to summon up her strength to once again act as if she wasn't crushed. She gathered her coat and her handbag, and then she spotted Sadie Johnson.

"Belle!" Sadie wove through the departing crowd. Her eyes were bright and her face flushed. "Wasn't that the most wonderful sermon?"

"It really was." She'd truly wished she could have absorbed more of it. Mary and Joseph's trust in the Lord was a lesson she needed right now, but her awareness of Brian remained. He stood, and she noticed. He spoke, and her soul listened. "Jeb is a fine minister."

"He's really amazing." Sadie glanced briefly toward the front of the church, where the young minister stood talking with Emmett and Carolyn. For a brief second, a wistful look passed across Sadie's face.

Was she in love with the minister? And why hadn't she noticed it before? Belle wondered. Probably because it took one to spot another. Belle could now say she was officially hopelessly in love. A secret she had to keep, but she could see it in Sadie.

"Mrs. Kettle loved it, and so did I." Sadie pulled the volume from her tote. "Thanks for letting us borrow it."

"You read the entire book to her?" Belle took the hardback thoughtfully. That had to have taken a lot of hours spent at the convalescent center.

"I didn't mind, it was fun and Mrs. Kettle almost feels like a grandmother," Sadie said with a touch of affection. A foster child growing up alone, she'd turned into a woman who understood loneliness in others and had a heart big enough to do something about it.

"You're coming to dinner with us, and this time I won't take no for an answer." Belle stepped into the aisle, making way for the rest of the family to follow. "Lupita made a big pot of chili, and now that Brian is heading back to Fort Worth—"

"He's l-leaving?" Sadie looked a bit alarmed.

"Don't worry, he'll be back for Christmas," Belle reassured her.

"And for the wedding." Lupita sidled in, looking lovely in a dark red dress. "It's decided. Christmas Eve afternoon. Our fine minister will be coming out to the Colby Ranch to perform the ceremony at four o'clock. Will that work?"

"Perfectly. We'll turn our Christmas Eve dinner into a celebration." Belle gave Lupita a hug. "This feels right. Your family is our family."

"Bless you. You have no idea what your support means." Lupita blinked, a hint of tears in her eyes. "I reminded my sister, Carolyn's mama, how well you've done and you've been in the same situation, Belle. I know it wasn't easy, but God worked great things with your life."

"Yes, He did." Infinitely grateful, she caught Sadie's hand before the girl could slip off unnoticed. "Lupita, do you know Sadie? She's coming home to eat with us."

"No, I wish I could." Sadie looked agitated and worried. She shoved her glasses into place. "I promised to stop by Ranchland Manor. They are having a Christmas party for family, and Mrs. Kettle invited me."

The girl could be stunning if she didn't work so hard to hide it. The baggy clothes, the unstyled hair. Belle wondered if there was any way to help the girl.

"Then you must come to the wedding," Lupita invited.

"Reverend Jeb will be there," Belle added, hoping that would be the deciding factor. She feared Sadie might spend Christmas Eve on her own, and this way she could make sure to include the girl in the Colby family celebrations. No one as kind as Sadie should be alone for the holidays. "I planned on dropping by the convalescent center. I have Christmas cookies to deliver. I'm going to invite some of the ambulatory patients to the wedding. Marjorie, Anna, Eunice and even Mrs. Kettle."

"Oh, I'd like that. I could help drive them,"

Sadie offered. The minister headed toward them, and Sadie flushed. "Well, I'd b-better get going."

"Goodbye, dear." It was hard not to feel motherly toward the girl. Belle watched her scamper off, determined to help her.

"Sadie left?" Violet tumbled into the aisle. "Too bad. I wanted to talk with her."

"But we were busy trying to talk Dad into staying," Maddie explained. "We failed."

"It was worth a try," Carter said as he joined them. "Hey, Jeb."

"Hi. Where did Sadie go off to in a hurry?" The handsome young minister searched the crowd and appeared disappointed there was no sign of her.

"She had a Christmas party to go to at Ranchland Manor," Belle explained, curious. Was Jeb interested in Sadie? She couldn't help wanting to matchmake, especially since love was not possible for her. Brian sat alone on the pew, his phone to his ear. Likely a professional call, perhaps about his hospitalized patient. She loved that he cared about people so much. One reason out of many why she adored him.

"Minister, it was a touching sermon." Brian shook Jeb's hand. "Thank you for it. I'm sorry, kids, but I have to go. My critical patient had a complication and she's in ICU."

Both sets of twins answered, expressing their

concern and offering prayers. Belle tried to do the same, but it was hard to speak with the rushing in her ears. She had to say goodbye to him. This was the moment she'd been dreading. She had to hold it together as Brian hugged his children, made promises for calls and vows to see each other soon. She forced a smile when inside she was dying.

"I'll keep your patient in my prayers," she told him when he turned to her. "Drive safely."

"I will." His hands found hers, his touch warm and connecting, like a current straight to her soul. "God keep you safe until we meet again."

This was not the end of the world, she told herself as he walked away. But it felt as if the sun went out, never to shine again, when he disappeared through the door.

This second heartbreak was a wound time would never heal.

Chapter Fourteen

"How are you girls doing in here?" Belle opened the door to her bedroom suite and set the tray on the small coffee table in the sitting area. "Carolyn, you look beautiful."

"Do I?" The sixteen-year-old studied her reflection in the mirror. She looked resplendent in her mother's wedding gown, the white lace adding a touch of femininity and the nipped-in waist emphasizing the teenager's willowy grace. "I don't feel like myself."

"That's because you are becoming someone more today." Carolyn's mother smiled beside her, tears in her eyes, tears of both concern and happiness. Clearly this had been hard news for the loving mother. "You will still be my precious daughter, but you are also to become a wife."

"It's so grown-up." Carolyn bit her bottom lip, worry stark on her youthful face. "I'm happy, but it's scary."

"The best things in life are," Belle assured her. "A little bit scary, a dash of exciting, but God is watching out for you, Carolyn."

"I'm trying to understand that," she said. "This is all so new, but it's going to be okay. Emmett and I love each other. You were glad you married Mr. Wallace, right, Belle?"

"Absolutely." She headed over to hug her daughters, who were fussing with Carolyn's hair, and noticed someone else in the chair in the far corner of the room. "Sadie! I didn't know you were here."

"Maddie spotted me and pulled me in here." Her too-large navy dress was clearly second-hand and better suited to a matron rather than a young woman in her twenties. "Is it time for me to head downstairs? I promised Mrs. Kettle I'd sit with her."

"There's plenty of time yet, and the last I looked, Lupita was keeping our friends entertained." Belle thought of Jeb and how he'd looked for Sadie in the crowd on Sunday. "Girls, you did a fantastic job with Carolyn's hair. She looks like a beauty queen."

"No, a cover model," Violet corrected.

"For *Vogue's* bridal issue," Maddie finished.

"Do you think Emmett will think so?" Carolyn blushed happily.

"We do," Belle assured her. "Girls, since it's

impossible for this bride to become any more beautiful, maybe you two could turn your attentions elsewhere."

"Elsewhere?" Violet's brow furrowed, not understanding.

"Oh, I see a likely candidate." Maddie shared a look with her twin. They nodded together in agreement and turned in unison to unsuspecting Sadie. "I have a dress that would look adorable on you."

"On me?" Sadie looked startled. "Oh, no, I mean, I couldn't. My dress is fine."

"And if we swept up your hair like this to show off your lovely face…" Violet slipped her fingers in Sadie's hair to demonstrate.

"And did some soft curls," Maddie chimed in. "Look at her. She'd be gorgeous."

"Exactly." Belle shared a smile with Carolyn, who nodded vigorously.

"Everything you need is right here," the teenager offered. "I think we have an extra flower we could put in Sadie's hair."

"Fun, fun, fun," Violet said.

"I'll run and get that dress." Maddie dashed off, leaving a red-faced Sadie behind.

"You shouldn't bother, honestly." She pushed her glasses up higher on her nose. "I don't need—"

"Let us do this for you," Violet said gently,

steering Sadie away from the chair and her big bulky handbag. "It's what friends do for each other."

"F-friends?" Sadie stuttered.

"Friends," Violet reassured her. "Mom, we're going to need that curling iron plugged in."

"I'm on it," she said, hurrying to comply. As she grabbed the cord, she felt something brush through her soul. She knew Brian had arrived even before she looked out the window and searched through the arriving crowd for him.

He had his duffel bag slung over one shoulder and carried a wrapped wedding gift. Seeing him distinguished in his black suit and tie hurt like an open wound. *You can do this,* she told herself. She could bury her feelings, gather her courage and face him as if they were nothing but an amicable divorced couple.

As if he could sense her, he turned toward the house and saw her in the window. His shoulders stiffened, his back straightened and a grim determination hardened his jaw. Was this as hard for him as it was for her? Something tore his attention away from her. He flashed her a look of apology before answering his cell. A beat passed while she watched him, unable to return her attention to the room. Was her heart showing? She feared it was.

"Mom? What do you think?" Maddie called

out as she zipped up Sadie. "Perfect color o
her, right?"

"Right." She leaned against the wall, puls
racing as if she'd run five miles. It was tough t
focus on Sadie, who truly did look pretty in th
sapphire-colored dress.

In the yard below, Brian's shoulders sank. H
pocketed his phone, looking weary, looking bea
It's not your business, she told herself, but tha
didn't stop her from wanting to go to him, t
find out what was wrong and hold him until th
sorrow on his face vanished.

"Wow, Carolyn, honey." Lupita appeared i
the doorway. "I've never seen a more beautifu
bride."

"Really?" the teenager asked hopefull
smoothing the satin skirt of her gown.

"Honest. Belle, I've told everyone to take
seat. Time to get this wedding started." Lupit
gave her niece a hug. "C'mon, baby. Emmett i
waiting for you."

"Emmett." Carolyn breathed his name, tru
love soft in her voice.

I remember being that young, Belle though
*So full of sweet, breathless love that the worl
seemed perfect. I remember being that bride.*

She looked out the window, but her Brian wa
gone from her sight. But from her heart?

Never.

* * *

"Dad, over here." Jack stood in the crowded living room, where the furniture had been moved and replaced with folding chairs. Evergreen garlands lined the walls and mantel, twinkle lights shimmered while red and white carnations scented the air. "We saved you a seat."

At the back of the arriving crowd, Brian nodded in affirmation. He needed the comfort of his family and was glad he'd come. But the call he'd received weighed on him. As a doctor, he dealt with life and sometimes with death. Grief plagued him as he waited while several ladies from the convalescent center clogged the aisle, trying to get settled.

"Brian." Belle's hand on his shoulder, her presence behind him. The sound of her voice was the balm his soul needed. "I can tell something is wrong."

He gazed into her brown eyes and read her wish to comfort him. She knew he was hurting without him needing to say a word. "Remember my patient with pneumonia who went into ICU on Sunday? She just passed away."

"I'm so sorry." Her arms came around him, drawing him against her slight form. She held him for a brief moment, as he breathed in the scent of shampoo in her hair and savored the

peaceful comfort only she could give him. "I
has to be so hard to lose a patient."

"Allie was our age." Brian swallowed hard
feeling alone when she released him and steppe
back. "Forty-three."

"She should have had so many years ahead o
her." Sorrow etched into Belle's face. "You sai
she was a grandmother."

"Of twin boys." He couldn't help casting a
glance through the crowd at Jack and Graysor
and Carter, sitting together, joking the way broth
ers did. "Think of all she will miss out on. Wed
dings, more grandchildren. Life."

"Love," Belle added.

Yes, love. Wasn't that what he was missing
out on? Allie's passing was a reminder. It was s
easy to lose those you loved. He and Belle ha
lost so much time together. If only he could hav
a second chance with her.

Did she feel this way, too? he wondered. Wa
she also afraid of reaching out? She stepped bacl
and avoided his gaze and he hoped she wante
to try again, but she was afraid. Just as he was

The string quartet, friends at church who ha
agreed to play, started the processional music
The ladies finally settled into their seats and th
aisle cleared.

Brian took Belle's hand. She didn't look a
him as she allowed him to accompany her thre

rows down to where their children sat waiting with their significant others.

"You're not using your cane." Brian couldn't hide his surprise.

"Ta-da!" She smiled, cheerful and happy, his Belle who could overcome anything. "After my physical therapy appointment this morning, I tossed my cane. Who needs it?"

"Especially after our marathon shopping trip on Thursday," Violet said as she slipped into one of the empty chairs.

"Yeah, Mom tired us out," Maddie explained as she took the last seat. On the top of the staircase, Carolyn appeared on the arm of Emmett's father.

"I'm so happy for them," Belle whispered to him, swiping tears from her eyes. "They aren't alone like we were. Their families are standing with them."

"They're going to be okay." They were so young, he thought, but he had faith that their love would see them through. He looked at Emmett, just a kid, standing straight and proud like a man. He remembered being that kid, so young, but just a kid.

Just a kid, he repeated to himself. A boy trying to do a man's job. And then it hit him, the perspective he'd never seen. He'd been just a teenager, trying to be a husband and provider and a father. That's all. Not a grown man, but a sixteen-year-old. Forgiveness filled him for the boy he'd been, who'd tried so hard.

He reached out to take Belle's hand and held on all through the ceremony.

"Lovely, just lovely." Marjorie Collins waylaid Belle in the aisle. She dabbed a lace-edged handkerchief at her eyes. "Such a pretty bride."

"Captivating," Anna Chandro agreed with a sniff. "Reminded me of my wedding. Roberto and I married young."

"So did me and my Charlie." Tears stood in Eunice Lundgrin's eyes. "We were happy for sixty-seven years."

"My John and I still are." Marjorie smiled. "Fifty-three years and going strong."

"Love is the greatest blessing," Anna agreed, smiling fondly at the newlyweds standing with their families and the minister in conversation. "It's what I wish for those two."

"Me, too." It was what Belle wished for everyone. Her gaze lingered on a resplendent Carolyn, clinging to Emmett's hand. The teenage boy stood strong, with his shoulders braced, ready to take on the world and determined to make his new bride happy.

The minister had invited the newlyweds to a support group at church. Jeb really was a fine reverend, a helpful man and quite good-looking. Wasn't it interesting how he would glance up and search the crowd covertly, as if he was seeking out a certain young lady?

Since her work for the day wasn't done, Belle excused herself, pointed her convalescent center cohorts in the direction of the dining room where Lupita was setting up a buffet and went in search of Sadie.

"Belle." Brian stepped out of the crowd, his nearness washing over her like peace. "Where are you going in such a hurry?"

"I'm looking for Sadie." Belle scanned the small crowd of friends, neighbors and family members chatting. No sign of the shy church secretary. "Maybe she's with the girls?"

"No, they are helping Lupita set out the meal." Brian shrugged his strong dependable shoulders. Did he have any idea how that made her want to step into his arms? To feel the quiet bliss whenever he held her?

"I wanted to do a little matchmaking, that's all." Her face heated. She was thankful Brian couldn't read her thoughts. "I think a certain minister is sweet on her. The girls gave her a little makeover, and I'd love for Jeb to see her. You wouldn't mind going on a little mission with me?"

"I have one of my own." His gaze raked over

her, as if searching for an answer to a question he hadn't asked. "You look radiant, Belle. You're happy."

"I am." She didn't jerk away when his hand cradled the curve of her face. She pressed her cheek into his palm, letting her soulful gaze meet his.

Hope. It lifted him higher than he'd ever been. He brushed a lock of auburn hair and folded it behind her ear. "Let's find Sadie, we'll complete your matchmaking mission and then we'll talk."

"It's a deal." She slipped her hand in his, right where it belonged. They belonged together. They always had. Seeing Emmett and Carolyn marry had reminded him of that.

"Maddie, we're looking for Sadie." He caught sight of his daughter and waved to her. "Have you seen her?"

"I thought she was heading to the kitchen to help," Maddie answered as she set out a coffee carafe. "But I haven't seen her since. I've been busy in here."

"Thanks." Belle kissed her daughter's cheek but didn't find Sadie in the kitchen.

"She was never here," Elise said, dishing food into a bowl at the stove.

"I didn't see her either," Savannah concurred as she poured potato chips into a big mixing bowl.

"I did." Keira removed the lid off a steaming

asserole fresh from the oven. "I saw her through
he doorway just passing by. It was strange, be-
ause she was walking away from the crowd. I
hought she was heading to the bathroom."

"Upstairs?" Belle asked.

"No. The one in the hallway near the den."
Keira shrugged. "I just assumed. Maybe she
eeded a break from the crowd."

"Thanks, Keira." Belle smiled, clearly glad
ack had fallen in love with this lovely young
voman. She was thankful her children had cho-
en well. She felt in her soul that their children's
utures would be happy ones, greatly blessed
vith love.

The family room was empty of anyone, echo-
ng faintly from the boom of conversations trav-
ling from the other end of the large house. The
athroom door tucked down the small hallway
vas visibly open. No obvious sign of Sadie.

"At least it's quiet here." Belle slid into a
earby chair as if she were seeking solitude.
More likely it was to take weight off her left leg
nd she was too stubborn to admit it.

"While we wait for Sadie to reappear, it might
e a good time to talk." He sat on the edge of
he coffee table, taking his time to search for
he right words, but what came out wasn't what
e intended to say. "I mailed a Christmas gift to
he Cruz family."

"The people who cared for you during your illness." Belle's fingers tightened around his. "I'm grateful to them. Without their kindness, we would have lost you. I can't bear to think about that."

"Neither can I," he confessed. "Today I'm thinking a lot about second chances and how we have to make the most of life. It's fleeting. You never know how much time you have with your loved ones, and the thought of a future without you in it—"

He stopped, overwhelmed with the kind of powerful, honest emotion that always before had shut him down. Although he'd been raised not to show emotion, not to show love, he'd finally overcome that. What he didn't have was a lot of practice revealing his entire soul. "Belle, I—"

Something thumped, a muffled sound, but distinct. Coming from the den. He pushed off the table, circled the couch and went to check it out. A young woman in a sapphire dress stood over his unzipped duffel bag with her hand inside it, her glasses magnifying her surprise and horror.

"Sadie." Belle's surprise echoed behind him. She pushed past him through the doorway and into the room. "What are you doing going through Brian's things?"

"I wasn't, I p-promise I wasn't doing anything b-bad." Sadie shook with emotion, her face crumpled and her gaze darted toward the door-way, her only escape. "I was just, well—"

"Leaving a Bible and a note?" Brian asked the frightened young woman gently.

"Y-yes," Sadie stuttered and buried her face in her hands.

Chapter Fifteen

"Sadie, you have been our mysterious gifter?" Belle couldn't get past the shock. "I don't understand. I've read the notes apologizing for separating our family. Sadie, you didn't do anything to us. We didn't know you until recently."

Tears streaked down the girl's face. "I came to Grasslands because you all were here."

"Because of us?" Violet and Maddie asked in unison. Belle saw their concern as they crowded through the doorway, side by side. Apparently they heard the commotion and rushed to the den to find out what was going on.

Sadie nodded. "I'd been able to find the Wallace half of the twins, but witness protection had changed your names so there was no record of it. I had no way to find the rest of you."

"How did you know we were in witness protection?" The shock began to wear off. Belle saw how distressed Sadie was, this girl who was faithful and devoted to her church, who volunteered at Ranchland Manor several times a week and who always seemed so alone. Sadie was a good person. So what was going on?

"You hunted them down…my children?" Brian asked sternly, clearly too upset to see the bigger picture. "I want to know why."

"T-to apologize." Sadie choked on a sob, looking like a young woman who had just lost her last hopes for any kind of happiness. "I followed Maddie to the café in Fort Worth, when you were in the nearby hospital with a coma, Belle. I wasn't trying to be creepy, I was trying to right a wrong. When I s-saw Violet, I followed her. That's how I f-found the rest of you."

"To give us the Bibles," Grayson clarified as he crowded into the room with Jack, apparently drawn by the growing crowd.

"Y-yes." She glanced over her shoulder, but there was no escape from the room.

"Your last name is Johnson," Belle remembered, laying a gentle hand on the girl's slender shoulder. "David Johnson was the man I saw kill someone, the reason why we went into witness protection. Do you know him?"

"He was my f-father." Sadie hung her head, overcome with shame. "Before he died, he accepted Christ into his heart and regretted what he'd done. He had begged me to deliver the Bibles and notes for him. He truly was sorry."

"Why didn't you just come out and tell us?" Belle asked quietly.

"Because you would see me differently. Just as you do now, don't you?" She took off her glasses to dry them with her sleeve. "I'm a m-murderer's daughter. It's what I've always been. It was so n-nice of you all to treat me like you did, like a real friend, like a regular person."

"That's why you never let anyone close?" Violet asked softly.

"Why you always ran away?" Maddie queried.

"I knew if the truth ever came out, then you wouldn't want to be my friend." Sadie squared her shoulders, as if resolved to face the family's rejection. But Jeb Miller, the minister, walked into the room, perhaps curious as to what was going on, and her face fell. She looked as if she'd lost her last dream. "N-no one could love me after that."

"You don't pay for your father's sins." Belle was sure of that. It wasn't right for this lovely young woman to feel condemned to loneliness. "You did nothing wrong, Sadie. In fact, you gave my family something so valuable, I will always be grateful to you."

"What do you mean? I don't understand." Hopelessness left her as if in shadow.

"You delivered the notes with Bibles, and it has allowed us to bury the past. We can focus on our future, all of us." She slid an arm around Sadie. "Even you."

"Me?" Confusion wreathed her pretty face.

"Bury the past with us, Sadie. Focus on this day the Lord has made and accept all the wonderful blessings He's given you." She glanced at Brian and saw her future in his eyes. They smiled together. "You have friends, you are a part of our church and you've made a home here. People care about you. Isn't that right, Jeb?"

"Absolutely." The young minister blushed, but his smile said it all. He was in love with the young lady. "Sadie, will you spend Christmas with me?"

"I'd like that." Sadie's face turned pink.

Belle gave the girl a hug, not at all surprised when Maddie and Violet joined in. Before she knew it, the Wallace-Colby family had gathered around Sadie, embracing her warmly and making her an honorary part of their family. After all, the same act of violence had destroyed Sadie's life, too. It was amazing how God had a way of making everything right in the end. Violet and Maddie reassured Sadie that all was forgiven, and Jeb looked like a man who had more to say to the woman he loved.

"What about us?" Brian asked, drawing Belle

into the kitchen, which had emptied out. The wedding guests were dishing up food in the dining room. Their merry conversations seemed a world away. He brushed a lock of hair from her eyes. "Maybe it's time for you and me to come clean, too."

"And talk about how we truly feel?" Tremors shot through her, both of anticipation and fear. It was scary looking your dream in the eye and knowing it was within your grasp. That your life was about to change for good and forever.

"Mom! Dad!" Violet tumbled into the kitchen.

"You'll never guess what." Maddie skidded into the room after her twin.

"Jeb proposed to Sadie." Jack stood in the doorway, with Carter and Grayson waiting behind him. "Right in front of everyone."

"And you missed it," Violet added. Her eyes widened, as if she realized something. "Oh, uh, you two are alone."

"Did we interrupt something?" Maddie demanded.

"No, no." Belle couldn't believe it. Twenty-five years later and the twins were still interrupting them. How funny was that? She took a step back, putting some space between her and Brian, giving her time to think. There were many things she needed to say. Well, there would be another time. "I'm happy for Sadie."

"We all are," Maddie agreed. "If you and Dad are busy—"

"No," Brian denied, but Belle could read the truth. She knew what he'd been about to say. So much hovered between them—dreams and prayers and hope. "No, we're fine."

"We'd better go get some food," Carter suggested. "It's going fast, and I'm starving."

"Me, too," Grayson and Jack said together.

"After you, Belle." Brian's hand settled on the small of her back, a light touch. Reassuring. The emotional connection between them deepened as she joined their children in the dining room. Happiness surrounded her as they toasted Emmett and Carolyn with sparkling grape juice and prayed for their happily ever after. During the prayer, Brian's hand found hers and held on tight, like a man who never wanted to let go.

There wasn't a chance to talk. Belle caught Brian watching her during dinner, a few times during kitchen cleanup before they raced to the church. The candlelight ceremony was lovely and inspiring. Sitting beside him was torture. Everything she wanted to say glowed so brightly within her she could hardly concentrate on anything else.

She hoped to grab a few moments alone with him once they returned home, but the kids were excited by their first Christmas together in decades. First there was chamomile tea and cookies to enjoy, then gifts to set out around the tree. So very many gifts, she realized with a shake of her head as she added her last package with the others. She'd gone a little overboard with her shopping, but it was a special Christmas, wasn't it? They were reunited for this holiday and for all the ones to come.

Brian hung back, as if waiting for her, but the girls were excited about Sadie's upcoming wedding and kept her company all the way to her room. Apparently Sadie had asked Violet and Maddie to be bridesmaids and they asked her to return the favor when it was their turn to say *I do*. The twins didn't settle down right away. Their voices kept coming from Violet's room, making it tough to slip undetected down the hall to find Brian.

So she went to bed. She tossed and turned, wondering if he was doing the same. The image of Carolyn as a bride stayed with her. The picture of Emmett so young and determined to be a man reminded her of Brian.

They'd both tried so hard against impossible odds. Two sets of twins were a great blessing and hugely stressful because they'd had no family support. They'd had no one to help, no one gathering around to celebrate their marriage or the children's births. No one to babysit for an hour or two, to turn to for advice, no one other than Brian's grandmother, who had been stoic and refused to help. *You made your bed,* she used to say. *Now you have to lie in it.*

Maybe if they'd had the support Emmett and Carolyn had, things would have been different. She rolled onto her side, watching the thin veil of moonlight fall through her window. Maybe she and Brian would have stayed together.

Maybe we have that chance now, she thought. She fell asleep with a smile on her lips and woke with it. She knew without words that Brian was up extra early, too. She slipped into the bathroom, changed into jeans and a Christmas sweater and pulled her hair into a ponytail. As she brushed her teeth, she saw someone she hadn't recognized in twenty-five years. A woman blushing and rosy, a woman in love.

Then she went down the stairs, careful not to make too much noise because the house and all her guests were sleeping. She found Brian in the living room. It was like stepping into a dream. The stillness of Christmas morning felt sacred as he turned from the mantel, where the children's stockings were hung in an orderly row.

"Putting in a few last-minute stocking stuffers?" She grabbed the end newel post and seemed to float off the last few steps.

"You caught me." With his hair sleep-tousled and dressed in an old gray sweatshirt and jeans, he couldn't look manlier. "I added a few surprises under the tree."

"You don't have to play Santa, Brian. It's likely our kids are old enough not to believe in him anymore." She didn't remember crossing the room.

"I wanted to put a few more surprises under the tree and in the stockings." His presence pulled her inexorably and suddenly she was in his arms, where she wanted to be. She laid her cheek against his chest.

"I did it for old times," he said, his voice rasping low. "And for new ones."

She prayed for many future Christmases spent together. It felt possible, within reach, tucked in Brian's arms. This is where she wanted to be forever.

A creak from somewhere in the house signaled they weren't alone. Belle stepped out of his arms just in time. Their grown children crept down the staircase, fresh-faced and happy, careful not to wake the others who were sleeping.

"Merry Christmas!" Violet padded up to hug Belle first, then Brian.

"Merry Christmas, sweetie." Belle took a moment to hug her daughter tight, and held out her arm to Maddie. She already had the best gift of all, as she then hugged her twin boys and Carter. Their talk filled the room, the girls turned on the tree lights and the boys discussed plans for distribution of presents after breakfast.

"Hey, what's this?" Grayson asked, standing in front of the mantel. "Dad, I recognize the envelope. Why did you put my DNA results in my stocking?"

"I thought we settled this." Jack joined him, tugging out the identical envelope from his Christmas stocking. "I know it in my heart. You're my father."

"We don't need to open the results," Grayson explained. "We love you, Dad. That's all that matters here."

"Your faith in me, well, it means everything." He was getting better at speaking his heart, Brian thought, and every day it would get easier. As the Christmas lights washed all of them with a rich glow, he took the envelope from Jack and tore it open. "Let's put the rumors to rest for good, shall we? I already know what this will say."

"I do, too." Belle's quiet words said much more to him. It felt as if they'd finally reached an understanding about the past, a past that no longer hurt, a past that was healed.

"I'm your dad." He handed Jack the paper verifying his paternity. "You're stuck with me now."

"I think I can handle that," Jack quipped. "But it's not news to me."

"Me, either," Grayson agreed. "Jack, what do you say we drag Carter with us and get the animals fed?"

"You read my mind, Gray." Jack folded up the paper and set it on the mantel. "We've got work to do, that's ranch life."

"The animals come first," Carter agreed, trailing after his big brothers. "Belle, we'll be back soon. Rumor has it that you make waffles every Christmas morning."

"You haven't lived until you've had my waffles." Belle winked.

"We'll get started in the kitchen," Maddie said. "There's coffee to make—"

"—and bacon to fry," Violet finished. "Although I'm thinking about link sausages, too."

"Good idea," Maddie agreed as they headed to the kitchen together. "When everyone wakes up and we're all gathered together, we're going to need a lot of food. No need to help us just yet, Mom—"

"Yeah, you and Dad finish whatever you were doing when we came down." Violet apparently had seen more than Belle had bargained on.

Oh, well. She shook her head, smiling when Brian did. "Apparently there's no hiding anything from those children of ours."

"No, they're pretty sharp. They must get that from you."

"No, definitely from you." Everything felt changed between them, full of possibilities. "We're finally alone."

"Yes, we are, and I have a few things to say." He tenderly trailed his fingertip across her temple, folding a lock of hair behind her ear. It was a gesture he'd done for her before, and so many times when they'd been married. His dark eyes deepened, letting her in all the way. There were no more barriers between them. "Remember when I walked into your room at the convalescent center for the first time? I didn't want to care about you again. I hardened my heart. No way was I going to get caught up in old feelings."

"I did the same." Her confession felt good, this sharing between them. She loved him. She always would. "I fought so hard against those old feelings."

"Me, too." His hand lingered against the side of her face, his touch so tender, she felt paralyzed. His dark eyes met hers and their breaths stilled, their hearts stopped. In that perfect moment there was only her love for him blazing brightly within her, sweet and pure and everlasting.

"At first I was afraid those old feelings were coming back." She pressed into his touch. Hopes lifted her as high as her most fervent prayers. "I feared they had the power to take over, but I finally realized that wasn't what was happening. My old feelings weren't coming back to life."

"They were brand-new." Tenderness seeped in his words, low and deep, and wrapped around her. His love was open and plain for her to see. He cradled her face in his hands. "I love you, Belle. My beautiful Belle. I don't know if I deserve someone as incredible as you, but I will spend every day of my life doing my best to make you happy."

"I love you, too." She felt closer than she'd ever been to him, to this Brian, new and improved, the man she'd dreamed he would be one day. She laid her hand on the hard plane of his chest. Infinite love swept through her, impossible to contain. "I'm so glad you want to be with me."

"Be with you?" He paused, shook his head and swallowed hard, as if he was overcome. As if he, too, couldn't believe they really had this second chance. "Belle, I want to marry you."

"What? Marry?" She couldn't have heard him right. He watched her with soulful, unblinking eyes, seeing deep into her heart where her great love for him lived. Happy tears stung her eyes. "Do you really think we can get it right this time?"

"Beyond all doubt." Certainty boomed in his

voice. "We are no longer kids, you and I. We can do better this time. Marry me, Belle. Say yes and make me the happiest man alive. Say yes and give me my only Christmas wish."

"Absolutely, positively yes." Tears rolled down her face, blurring the sight of him. "I would love to marry you. I think we were meant to be."

"Always and forever." He towered over her, her wonderful man, and brushed her tears from her cheeks with the pads of his thumbs. "Do you know what this means?"

"That we'll finally get our happily ever after?" Her gaze sparkled with precious love for him.

"Our happily ever after starts right now." A brand-new future spread ahead of them. One full of weddings and grandchildren and their love deepening day by day, year by year, all the way to eternity. "I will cherish you for the rest of my life, Belle."

"As I will cherish you," she promised. "We finally have the fairy tale. The dream I had when I first fell in love with you."

"It only took us two tries to get it right." He pulled her into his arms and tucked her lovingly against his chest. "We are very blessed indeed."

"That we are." Her eyes grew luminous as he leaned in and kissed her tenderly. Her lips brushed his and it was perfection. Flawless, the way true love's kiss should be.

Epilogue

Four months later

"It's a perfect day for a wedding." Belle squinted up into the April sunshine falling like a halo around the white-steepled church. Birds sang, flowers bloomed and the diamond ring on her hand sparkled like the joy within her. "On a day like this, without a cloud in sight, it feels like a promise from above. Sadie and Jeb's happiness seems guaranteed."

"It sure does. Love is the greatest blessing." Brian draped his arm around her shoulder, drawing her against him. Happiness looked amazing on him, and so did his black suit and tie. "And we have been doubly blessed. Twice."

"And then some," Belle agreed, waving at Carter, who stood near the church entrance with his hand pressed against the small of Savannah's back, gently guiding her. Baby Hope lay cradled in her mother's arms, fast asleep. They'd been married in a family-only ceremony in late January. The glow of true love surrounded them.

"We'll save you a spot," Carter called above the last-minute crowd rushing to the church. No one wanted to be late for Sadie's wedding.

"Sounds good." Sweet spring breezes stirred through her hair and ruffled the hem of her dress. She remembered her own January wedding to Brian on a day as sunny as this. One of the best days of her life.

"Hi, Belle!" Ty Garland headed toward them through the crowd, with pretty little Darcy at his side. "Hi, Brian. It's strange to arrive without my better half."

"Who is a bridesmaid," Belle pointed out. And soon to be a bride herself. Their wedding date was set for the first of May…just around the corner. She couldn't wait to see her final child happily married.

"Hey, there's Landon." Ty waved to a man with sandy-blond hair heading their way. "Do you think Violet can get through the ceremony with her morning sickness?"

"That's the hope." A happily married man, Landon loped over. He and Violet had tied the knot in a romantic Valentine's Day wedding, and Violet's immediate pregnancy was another blessing to the Wallace family.

Life is good, Belle thought as she accompanied her husband and her sons-in-law into the church. Carter waved from the bride's side of the church, filled with the many people who had come to know and love Sadie. Sadie was clearly no longer alone and never would be. Marjorie, Anna and Eunice waved from their pew near the front, along with Mrs. Kettle. Belle waved back.

"Mom, Dad." Grayson stood, looking dashing in his suit and tie. "Can you believe how crowded it is?"

"Not at all." She kissed her son's cheek. "Sadie is treasured by everyone she meets. Oh, there's the processional music. We arrived just in time."

"Come sit beside me," Elise invited, patting the bench beside her. She and Grayson had married in a candlelight service on New Year's Eve. Cory, now officially her grandson, rushed up to take her hand.

"You can sit by me, too," he offered.

"Why, I would love that." Belle cast a glance at Brian. "I'm afraid a more handsome young man has come between us."

"That's all right." Brian ruffled Cory's hair affectionately. The boy smiled up at his new grandfather. "It means that I get to sit with him, too."

Cory settled between her and Brian on the bench. Sweet Darcy swirled over in her fancy dress and scooted in. Life was much, much better with grandchildren, Belle decided. Icing on the best cake ever. She loved her family.

"Belle, how is Violet feeling this morning?" Keira's wedding ring glinted as she leaned across Elise and Grayson on the narrow pew. She and Jack had whisked everyone to Oklahoma for a family elopement last month. As newlyweds, neither Keira nor Jack seemed able to stop smiling.

"Prayers would be appreciated, she said," Belle answered. "I called to check in on her about thirty minutes ago. She said so far, so good."

"Prayers will be coming," Keira promised as the crowd hushed and the flower girl, Jeb's niece, skipped down the aisle tossing rose petals.

"Mom." Jack kept his voice low, so it wouldn't carry. "You and Dad look especially happy this morning."

"We certainly do." Every day with Brian had been a blessing. Every day had only proven to her how right she'd been to let him closer, let him in and risk loving him again. He'd taken Doc Garth's offer and set up his practice at the Grasslands Medical Clinic. He'd decided to pare down his missionary work to one trip a year and concentrated on offering help where he could in their community. Which meant she and their children saw much more of him.

"How about you?" she asked him. "You look happy enough to burst."

"That's because my life is perfect," Jack confessed, slipping his arm around his bride. He'd officially changed his last name to Wallace, since it was his rightful name.

Maddie was the first to waltz down the aisle, resplendent in lilac. Her hair was tucked into a small flowered tiara, and she looked like a princess parading by. She paused to search out Ty in the crowd, and the look they shared radiated pure love.

Violet followed her in a lavender gown. A pretty blush painted color across Violet's face when she found her husband in the crowd. True love made her even more beautiful. Landon pressed his hand to his heart, a silent message of his feelings for her.

The music changed, the crowd stood and Belle took a moment to help both Darcy and Cory to their feet. It was bliss to be a grandparent, she thought. As Brian's gaze met hers, she knew he was thinking the same thing.

Across the aisle, a movement caught her eye. Carolyn waved cheerfully, her small baby bulge showing beneath her dress. Happiness lit her up, and she was surrounded by her family. Her mother, her aunt Lupita and both of Emmett's parents. Emmett stood beside her, holding her hand, a man determined to always stand by her.

Sadie entered the sanctuary, holding a bouquet of lavender roses, her wedding dress flowing around her. As lovely as she was, her purity of heart shone through. She glanced down the aisle and the moment she saw Jeb waiting for her, she lit up. Nothing was more beautiful than a woman truly in love. Belle felt so thankful for Sadie that she could barely breathe as the young woman swished by.

"Have I told you today how much I love you?" Brian drew close to whisper.

"Only five times." Joy filled her as their gazes locked. So much everlasting love gleamed in his eyes, it was without measure and without end.

So was her love for him.

Thank You, Father. She cast her gaze upward to the rafters, knowing He could hear her. She could feel His touch in her life and on her soul. Life was good. Her children were reunited and happy. Their futures looked amazing.

And thank You for Brian, she added. Her life was perfect. All the bliss she'd ever dreamed of as that sixteen-year-old bride had come true.

"Dearly beloved." The minister's voice rang through the sanctuary, piercing Belle's thoughts. She blinked and found Brian smiling at her.

"You are my beloved, for now and forever," he whispered and took her hand.

* * * * *

Dear Reader,

It's been such a pleasure working on the Texa
Twins stories. Writing continuities such as thi
one is a much different experience than writ
ing a book by yourself, as you can imagine. I
involves a lot of emailing back and forth be
tween my fellow authors, and it's been an hono
working with Kathryn Springer, Glynna Kaye
Arlene James, Barbara McMahon and Mart
Perry. I hope you've enjoyed the enfolding stor
of the Wallace-Colby family as they delve int
their parents' past and find true love along th
way.

Reunited for the Holidays is the final install
ment of the family's saga, where Brian return
from his extended absence to discover that hi
ex-wife is awake from her coma and their twin
have found each other. But that's just the start o
his worries. What about the past? Are they stil
in danger? Can he and Belle make things wor
as civilly divorced parents? Who is the mysteri
ous gifter who has been leaving the Bibles an
notes? And the biggest question of all—will th
old rumors about him and Belle finally be put t
rest? I hope you enjoy finding out these answer

as Brian and Belle journey toward the love and forgiveness God means for them.

Wishing you love and grace this Christmas season,

Jillian Hart

Questions for Discussion

1. What are your first impressions of Brian? How would you describe his character? What do you like about him?

2. What are your first impressions of Belle? What do you learn about her from the way she treats others—including her children, her ex-husband and those around her in the convalescent center? What does this tell you about her character?

3. Brian has been guilty of keeping his heart closed and not showing his feelings. Why is this? What impact has this had on his life and relationships? How does he try to change? What does this say about him?

4. How does Belle feel about Brian's help at the beginning of the book? How does this change as she spends time with him again? How does spending time with him change her?

5. How hard must it have been for Belle to give up two of her children? How hard was it for Brian? They each went on with their lives in different ways. Brian remarried. Belle

never did. What does this say about each of their characters?

6. When does Belle begin to realize she is falling in love with Brian again?

7. What do you think of Brian's relationship with his children? How does it change him through the book?

8. What are Belle's strengths? What are her weaknesses? What do you come to admire about her?

9. What are Brian's strengths? What are his weakness? What do you come to admire about him? How do you know he will be a good husband to Belle?

10. What changes Brian's mind about not deserving Belle's love? What makes him forgive himself?

11. What values do you think are important in this book?

12. What do you think are the central themes in this book? How do they develop? What meanings do you find in them?

13. How does God guide both Brian and Belle? How is this evident? How does God lead them to true love?

14. There are many different kinds of love in this book. What are they? What do Brian and Belle each learn about true love?

LARGER-PRINT BOOKS!

GET 2 FREE
LARGER-PRINT NOVELS
PLUS 2 FREE
MYSTERY GIFTS

Love Inspired

Larger-print novels are now available...

Love Inspired® SUSPENSE

RIVETING INSPIRATIONAL ROMANCE

Watch for our series of edge-
of-your-seat suspense novels.
These contemporary tales
of intrigue and romance
feature Christian characters
facing challenges to their faith...
and their lives!

AVAILABLE IN REGULAR
& LARGER-PRINT FORMATS

For exciting stories that reflect traditional values,
visit:
www.ReaderService.com

FAMOUS FAMILIES

YES! Please send me the *Famous Families* collection featuring the Fortunes, the Bravos, the McCabes and the Cavanaughs. This collection will begin with 3 FREE BOOKS and 2 FREE GIFTS in my very first shipment— and more valuable free gifts will follow! My books will arrive in 8 monthly shipments until I have the entire 51-book *Famous Families* collection. I will receive 2-3 free books in each shipment and I will pay just $4.49 U.S./$5.39 CDN for each of the other 4 books in each shipment, plus $2.99 for shipping and handling.* If I decide to keep the entire collection, I'll only have paid for 32 books because 19 books are free. I understand that accepting the 3 free books and gifts places me under no obligation to buy anything. I can always return a shipment and cancel at any time. My free books and gifts are mine to keep no matter what I decide.

268 HCN 0387   468 HCN 0387

Name _____ (PLEASE PRINT)

Address _____ Apt. #

City _____ State/Prov. _____ Zip/Postal Code

Signature (if under 18, a parent or guardian must sign)

Mail to the **Reader Service**:

IN U.S.A.: P.O. Box 1867, Buffalo, NY 14240-1867
IN CANADA: P.O. Box 609, Fort Erie, Ontario L2A 5X3

* Terms and prices subject to change without notice. Prices do not include applicable taxes. Sales tax applicable in N.Y. Canadian residents will be charged applicable taxes. This offer is limited to one order per household. All orders subject to approval. Credit or debit balances in a customer's account(s) may be offset by any other outstanding balance owed by or to the customer. Please allow 4 to 6 weeks for delivery. Offer available while quantities last. Offer not available to Quebec residents.

Your Privacy— The Reader Service is committed to protecting your privacy. Our Privacy Policy is available online at www.ReaderService.com or upon request from the Reader Service.
We make a portion of our mailing list available to reputable third parties that offer products we believe may interest you. If you prefer that we not exchange your name with third parties, or if you wish to clarify or modify your communication preferences, please visit us at www.ReaderService.com/consumerschoice or write to us at Reader Service Preference Service, P.O. Box 9062, Buffalo, NY 14269. Include your complete name and address.